MOTHER BITCH AND BITCH MOTHER

MOTHER BITCH AND BITCH MOTHER

SEAD MAHMUTEFENDIĆ

Mother Bitch and Bitch Mother

Copyright © 2024 by Sead Mahmutefendić. All rights reserved.

No part of this publication may be reproduced, stored in a retrieval system or transmitted in any way by any means, electronic, mechanical, photocopy, recording or otherwise without the prior permission of the author except as provided by USA copyright law.

The opinions expressed by the author are not necessarily those of URLink Print and Media.

1603 Capitol Ave., Suite 310 Cheyenne, Wyoming USA 82001
1-888-980-6523 | admin@urlinkpublishing.com

URLink Print and Media is committed to excellence in the publishing industry.

Book design copyright © 2024 by URLink Print and Media. All rights reserved.

Published in the United States of America

Library of Congress Control Number: 2024904531
ISBN 978-1-68486-711-0 (Paperback)
ISBN 978-1-68486-714-1 (Digital)

22.02.24

Library
SELECTED WORKS

Editor
Almir Zalihić

Reviewers
Prof. Daniejela Bačić-Karković, PhD
Sead Begović, author
Prof. Igor Štiks, PhD Amir Brka, author
Ivan Pandžić, author
Šaban Šarenkapić, author
Željko Grahovac, author
Prof. Senadin Lavić, PhD
Branko Čegec, author
Almir Zalihić, author

1.

I hear her laughter.
I'm moving.
The laughter stops.
A child is crying somewhere upstairs.
Enza's hand is hot and moist, ruddy as a sponge, with dimples at the root of each finger. The gal wears thick glasses that make her eyes look like those of a fish.
It's raining outside. On the lower floor, Semiz is arguing with someone.
All that Enza had of luggage were a suitcase and a plastic bag with two wooden hangers jutting out of it.
The smell of her sweat permeates the room. Her back is huge.
Thick pink legs, tapering and squeezing into small shoes made of cheap leatherette, can be seen under the chair.
Enza and Semiz are lying in bed. Enza is lying on her back with her arm outstretched, while Semiz, snuggled up to her side, is lying on her arm.
Enza does not like to cook. She prefers to dress up and go out. She could talk on the phone for hours.
Enza always looks sad when talking to little Ra and telling him what to do. She does it very noisily and nervously as if she is reluctant to talk to him.
After that, she laughs frantically to herself. It looks, in fact, as if she does not want to exist.
Upstairs, Ra begins to cry. Enza leaves, brings him downstairs and puts him on her lap.
Ra looks nothing like Enza. The little boy has dark brown hair and ears that are too big for his head.
Enza's mother Paula offers to place Ra on her lap.
Ra screams from Enza's arms and points his finger at the bitch Tita. Tita is pregnant. She will be whelping soon.

When Ra finds himself on Paula's lap, the child calms down instantly. Probably because it is the biggest and softest lap in the whole world.

Paula entertains little Ra on her lap very nicely. She plays with his knees as if galloping. Ra is screaming and hopping all the time, asking for more.

Enza watches them play with the same expression she might have if she were watching television.

Paula carries Ra to his mother. Ra does not want to be separated from his grandmother, screaming, "mo, mo, mo!"

He screams like that for five more minutes until Enza, in her anger, gives him a hot slap.

Then she throws a deflated bag on her shoulder and runs out like some kind of fury.

2.

The window is wide open.

The room is filled with fresh morning air. Only one picture covers the bare walls.

It is to the left of the window.

The picture is in color, taken from some illustrations.

Two children are running along the seashore holding hands. The sun is setting. Everything in the picture is dark red.

Even the children.

Semiz waits for Enza standing by the door. He watches as she squeezes her round pink feet into small flat shoes. He then watches as she combs her very short hair with a brush, which has a small ellipse-shaped mirror on the back.

She has orange lipstick on her lips.

That lipstick is as glittery as a traffic sign.

Enza sings. Semiz is in the back yard. From there, he listens to her voice while trying to assemble the bike from parts and pieces.

Her voice can be heard through the open window.

Enza doesn't know the words to the song. She sings la-la-la, laa-a. Her singing resounds throughout the house.

She will never say that there is something she does not know, Semiz thought with indignation. She likes to sing the most when she is in the kitchen.

After lunch, she shows Semiz a photo of her mother Paula and her Italian father, whom she doesn't even remember.

She is between the two of them. Squinting in one eye from too much sun.

I'm the only fat one, says Enza.

Everyone is smiling in the photo, because dad was fooling around to make them laugh.

I'm fat both when I laugh and when I'm angry, Enza continues to spout into Semiz's ear.

She goes on telling him about the time when children laughed at her for being so fat. Semiz just nods without any reply.

He still thinks that she would never say that there is something she does not know.

Enza does not wear jeans and Indian shirts, probably because she cannot find the right size for herself, her buttocks, breasts, hips and thighs.

That's why she usually wears loose floral-fabric dresses.

But when she gets upset about something, she laughs in a peculiar way. This is what Semiz calls Enza's patent. She pinches her nose to prevent a short and convulsive fit of laughter. Her huge and ruddy hands tremble and strain to breathe in some air.

If her acquaintances are around her, then everyone thinks she is mentally ill, and Enza usually looks away. As soon as they look into her eyes, they burst into even stronger and louder laughter until their loins start aching, so they would most like to stop.

They still think it is because of her cute fatness.

Some of them pull her leg, calling her the Slender Angel. While the others are laughing.

It is not that they are hostile towards her.

Semiz is the only one who understands the whole thing. He best knows how sad Enza is in these moments, so when they finally remain alone, he calls her Tristezza.

You are my Tristezza.

You're the only one who knows how to get into someone else's state, she tells him gently.

3.

On one occasion, Enza asked Semiz what he thought about hashish.

Sometimes, in the evenings, the group would sit and smoke hashish in Oly's hookahs and listen to the stereo set at full blast.

That same afternoon, Enza was photographed with little Ra in her arms and pregnant Tita lying down between her fat, pink legs. She is leaning against the kitchen door jamb. She is squinting a little from the sun, just like the little girl from that long-ago photograph between her parents, mom Paula and Italian dad, whom she hasn't even truly remembered.

Enza photographs Semiz riding a bicycle behind the house. He doesn't keep his hands on the handlebars so as to show off.

The bike has just been assembled from parts and pieces. Bitch Tita is also there. Poor thing, her teeth gritted. She does not trust the camera.

EVERYTHING HUMAN IS FOREIGN TO ME.

When Semiz clicked and flashed, little Ra stretched out his arms towards him from his mother's embrace and screamed, "mo, mo".

Ra screams on Paula's lap and scatters breakfast over the kitchen table. Enza runs in, grabs him and slaps him with all her might. The child runs out of breath. His face turns blue.

Completely mute. Getting into shock.

In the hall, Semiz is having a long and extensive discussion about some nonsense with someone over the phone.

He ends it up babbling.

He comes to them in the room noisily and with wild gestures.

He then takes a book off the shelf. He tries to read.

It is clear that he is angry and that he cannot even concentrate on what should be called reading.

No one speaks for a while. Paula's knees try lulling little Ra so that he would not cry.

In vain.

"She won't, she won't", his grandma tells him tenderly. "Oh no, mom, you're not going to touch little Ra. Take this, mom, grandma will beat mom!"

"Stop twaddling", she politely and gently addresses her mother.

Semiz then gets up. He leaves the apartment. Enza gets up too.

HIS FAITHFUL LOVE FOLLOWS HIM.

She too finds herself in the January bora.

All the while, Ra continues to scream for Enza. In front of him is a book with illustrations, which Paula flips over to him in a panic because of the two of them, and seemingly marvels and admires what is inside, "Ah, look at the bear! Wow, a cow! Behold the horns! Prick-prick!"

4.

You ask me what I did when I saw you. Well, let me tell you: I masturbated.

You think I'm nasty and perverted?

After that I washed my hands, which is more than other people do.

And I felt better.

Do you understand what I mean? I burst into tears. The way things were going here in this room, what else was left?

That's fine when it comes to you.

I bet you live in a clean room and that your wife washes your bedding.

You cannot do me any good, except hearing me out.

All I wanted was to have children. When Enza was born, I wanted to be the child I always wanted. I tried to stop her from growing and I succeeded in that for a long time.

You know, I did not teach her to speak until she was ten.

I did not send her to school, I kept her at home with the excuse that it was a dangerous neighborhood.

I hugged her day and night.

I did not like it when Enza outgrew the cradle. I went and bought a crib at a public hospital sale.

There, I used to do things like that.

I did not let her do anything by herself. I even prevented her from doing any cleaning so she would not get dirty.

I used to barely get around without her and she adored it.

It took her a long time to get dressed in the morning.

And if only you could see how clumsy she was with knife and fork. I'd rather have someone come, pat her on the shoulder, and spoon-feed her.

Can you believe me?

That's why I spit on my daughter, even though I made her that way.

I'm thirty-six, she's fifteen. I am still an attractive woman. Many people flatter me that I'm younger.

If only I were free from this obsession with her, I could easily get married. I am so consumed with trying to get her back into my womb.

That's how it was until I met you. Then everything changed thoroughly.

One obsession replaced another overnight.

Now all the missed sex has caught up with me. I'm just crazy about you as if I weren't crazy enough already.

I have already started beating her son Ra if he spills food or mispronounces words.

Enza goes out more often in the evening, leaving me alone at home.

I have started to suffer from severe headaches. My arms and legs simply stop obeying me. The tongue behaves as if it belongs to someone else, not me.

A true nightmare.

Everything is becoming black like hell.

I'm lying in my own shit in this dark house.

5.

Semiz continues to paint in his own manner. He begins to see things the way he felt them.

He tries to paint himself.

Some strange yellow and white shapes come out.

After that, he paints his mother.

She, on the other hand, is represented with a huge red mouth across the entire canvas.

It's her lipstick.

He painted the mouth black.

It's because he hated her.

Enza finds it difficult to get out of bed in the morning. It's better to stay under the covers. She is safe there.

She gets anxious just thinking about facing thousands of people, ear-splitting city traffic, queues, and similar things.

She begins to remember those old times when she was with her mother, that old life, when everything was nestled, when everything was done for her, when everything was warm and safe.

6.

I think that these attacks became less frequent because Enza brought Semiz home one day. She presented me to him as if I was mentally disabled.

He was dead, and even had long hair, slicked back.

He always wore a black suit, and underneath it a black T-shirt with a high collar.

He claims to be a painter.

And what's more – a painter and a half.

Thus successful, he came to hate me on sight.

I also came to hate him because he snatched Enza from me.

Literally - snatched.

Scoundrel!

The first time he just nodded when Enza introduced him to me, and after that he never addressed a word directly to me.

He didn't even notice me.

Full of himself — I am one hundred percent sure — he could not stand that people like me even exist.

He came to our apartment quite regularly to take Enza somewhere in the evening.

I watched television. I felt quite lonely then. With the evening program ending, I would usually sit in the kitchen and wait for Enza.

I cried a lot then.

Semiz stayed with us more and more often, until he completely moved in with us.

One afternoon, the two of them spruced up, got dressed and went out somewhere.

When they returned late that night, better said in the still of the night, they guffawed in the hallway. Then they behaved with abandon all over the apartment. They must have been quite drunk.

That night Enza told me that the two of them had gotten married.

I had an attack, the worst one up until that moment.

It seemed like it lasted for days, even though it lasted only an hour or two, or something like that.

When the attack passed, I opened my eyes. I saw the expression on Enza's face.

It was utterly disgusting.

How much a person can change in a short time!

When I saw that expression, I immediately realized that for me she is the same as some total stranger, like — let's say — her father when he left us.

I stayed with them for three months until they found a home to put me there. They were too absorbed in each other to notice me.

They were even barely addressing me at all.

I was quite happy when I left the place, even though it was my dream.

I even cried a little when I was leaving.

I guess they were glad to see my back.

It was not bad in the home to which they took me.

Actually, I didn't even care where I was.

7.

I am beginning to think that my mother got fed up with the man she had married, so if I go back to Bosnia, we will continue as before. Well, that had been going on in my head for days until it turned into an obsession.

I don't think of anything else. I convinced myself that she was expecting me.

She will hug me and spoon-feed me.

One evening, Semiz thought about it, so he decided to go to her.

What was I waiting for?

I ran outside.

I ran through the streets the whole way.

I was almost singing for joy.

I caught the train.

When I arrived, I ran home from the station.

Everything will be fine again.

There was light on the lower floor.

I rang the bell.

I felt, all of a sudden, that I was unsteady on my feet so I had to lean against the wall.

The person who came to the door was a girl.

She didn't know what to say.

The stupid silence went on while she was thinking of what to say to me.

Then the girl asked Semiz who, in fact, he was? He told her that he was looking for his mother.

Selma Mulabećirović.

"She passed away two years ago", replied the girl.

Her words were like a surgical knife. Semiz stared past her down the hall.

Everything is really different now. He is overcome with sadness at this change. He feels cheated.

He wants the girl to invite him inside, to the warm room, to just embrace him and say, "Come live with us."

Thus he thought while walking back towards the station.

8.

Selma is lying on a divan in the virgin forest. Her upper part of the body is half raised and supported by the right hand. Two black braids are hanging on the side. Her legs are crossed as if her ankle joints are tied in a knot.

The line of her hips is very curved.

Her lap is smooth and small.

Her breasts are regular and sphere-shaped.

She is looking to the right, out of the painting.

To the left, an outstretched arm is pointing in that direction.

She is dreaming with her eyes open.

Dangerous tigers are lurking cunningly and curiously from the bushes. Beneath the tall lotuses are ferns and bushes with sword-shaped leaves.

The trees form a curtain that goes up to the sky. Somewhere there is a small waterfall.

Snakes and birds are hidden.

A hungry lion is tearing an antelope to pieces. A jaguar is attacking a horse.

Baboons are funny pranksters.

Selma is lying on a divan in the virgin forest and dreaming with her eyes open.

9.

He slowly makes his way through the cold rain. Semiz senses that Enza is in a bad mood.

When he entered the apartment, he was met with raised eyebrows and a slightly contemptuous look.

He still kept his hands in his pockets.

He walked down the hall in silence.

The impression is even stronger because of the subdued light, which was barely penetrating the curtains and the damp morning that was creeping into the room.

It was cold and his teeth were chattering.

He could feel her bitterness.

He left the apartment.

He crossed the street.

The cold air hit his face again, and the pestering raindrops were sticking to his suit.

He managed to overcome the chaos of feelings in which he found himself.

He breathed in the icy morning air, allowing it, with a certain satisfaction now, to fill up his entire lungs.

His expression was impersonal, and his gaze unwavering.

He saw this in the shop-window of a glass store, where he spotted his figure with huge dark circles under the eyes in an oval mirror.

He promised himself that he would get a good sleep the next night.

10.

Our bodies were motionless. Your hand caressed my breasts a few more times before moving down to my belly, thighs, hips, and down there...

Everything was burning inside me. Tiny stars were twinkling before my eyes.

I felt your tears that had completely soaked my hot face.

You kissed me with such ferocity, which I would never have expected.

Your hands roamed roughly over my body.

Our bodies then intertwined.

We sobbed, looking for a way to free ourselves from our clothes.

When you left, my whole body was numb for a while.

The silence filled me with fear.

I inhaled as deeply as I could.

I was hitting the furniture.

My hands were eagerly groping. I still felt your warmth in my empty hands.

I wished to fall asleep so that I would never move and to forget in this room how time passes.

I'm saying that it's what I have to get into so that I could get out.

11.

Enza sits tilting her head towards Semiz to hear him better.
What's the deal with her? – he thought.
She watches him with her wet eyes, and is on the verge of bursting into tears.

12.

Three days later, completely joyous, she welcomes him, bathed, in a rust-colored silk robe, her cheeks more apple-like than ever before.

She knows how to smile mischievously.
And there are dimples when she smiles.
She knows how to combine laziness and ambition.

13.

I saw you. I almost screamed.
You looked at me with a deep and mysterious gaze.

14.

Semiz was gifted, but he was not up to the temptations that came with unemployment.

15.

I'm going.
Someone is knocking on the door.
Who is it, Semiz growled.

Police!

Damn, cursed Semiz.

Open or we're breaking in!

Enza is trying to get dressed as fast as she can.

Go to hell, we didn't do anything.

How come you didn't, isn't there a minor in there?

Are you a minor? Semiz asks her.

No, she replies.

There isn't! – shouted Semiz to those in front of the door.

How come there isn't, open it or we'll open it!

So open it!

The door opened wide. One guy in civilian clothes and a policeman in a uniform.

Enza was just finishing getting dressed.

is your name? – the civilian asked Enza.

Semiz answered instead, "The lady's name is Enza. Mrs. Enza Litzow."

Miss Litzow, in fact, are you a Miss, I mean, are you still a minor?"

Miss Litzow, said the policeman, you are a minor.

If you say so, sir. I'm fifteen years old and don't you yell at me because it jars on my boyfriend's ears.

Semiz and Enza slowly got out. They didn't even try to keep them.

When they reached the street, they both broke into a desperate run.

When they reached the end of the street, they stopped.

No one was following them.

Why are we running? – Enza asked.

Just because, Semiz replied.

What do you mean, just because?

They came to the Municipality. They had to wait for the judge for half an hour. When he arrived, Semiz addressed him, "This young lady is already twenty years old and has had three abortions. I'm twenty. Of course, Mr. Judge, the plain truth is that we live common-law and have a child, actually a six-month-old boy, and we want to end this inappropriate situation, much to the relief of her religious mother. We also have a thousand marks."

And your documents? – the municipal clerk asked him.

I have already told you, Your Honor, we have a thousand marks.

Judge: Why did you come to Croatia?

Semiz: You will not believe me if I tell you that I came in here to put it in my ass. (He's talking back to that strapping guy from the South, who was just stretching his wrists to acquire the state-building behavior.)

The clerk raised a pandemonium, screaming "It will always be like this in Croatia!"

Semiz advised the state-building body to calm down and that he was not attacking Croatia, but wanted to defend it from such fools.

Do you know, Mussie, that we can nab you for insulting a representative of public order or that we can keep you as long as we want?

Wow, tonight's gonna be the night, Semiz yawned, but he immediately backed away before those two state-building eyes, which informed him that they were as dangerously close to him as the lights of a locomotive entering a tunnel at night, and which would reduce him to a pile of swallowed wishes at any moment, which suddenly made Semiz a hogwash of rage and humiliation so that he became unclear, dark and smelly to himself. His fleshy mouth, long and slightly asymmetric nose, and his bat ears sticking out through the back-slicked hair, came to the fore even more.

He revealed his teeth, yellowed with tartar.

The judge laughed.

He explained to Semiz like this, you see, you won't be able to get married that way in Rijeka. No way. Priest. Capeesh! If you don't know Italian by any chance.

It's out of the question, Semiz yielded. We haven't lost anything by trying, have we?

The sun is getting stronger and stronger outside.

Enza took off her coat.

Sem, she said, I'll have to ask mom for permission and all that.

Are you or are you not a minor? – he asked.
Of course I am.

16.

Semiz hated money. As soon as he received an advance payment for a painting, which he hadn't even painted yet, he would spend it immediately, so he borrowed money every day until he got paid. He would carefully write down the names of the creditors on the closet door and would pay them back as soon as he got the rest of the money.

He would stand by the cash desk and distribute to each one as much as he owed them.

Before that, he would take photos of the closet door that had the names of those he owed.

After that, he would laugh with the rest of the money, not knowing what to do with it.

What to do with this?

Throw it in the fire or squander it.

INTO THE FIRE, OR THE FLAME?

Of course, he would spend it all on the same day, so he had to borrow money for the bus on the way home.

17.

When they brought the first pints of beer, they took the foam with their hands and smeared it on their faces and hair.

Everyone was furious, irritated and half-drunk. A few beers were enough to put them to sleep.

No one had money for a more luxurious fix.

Saving money meant spending six months without grog or any similar comfort.

There were no more suicidal falls from the roofs, buildings and bridge railings. They were falling like overripe fruit from the rotten trees in some forgotten orchard.

They were overcome by a sense of immense loss.

They longed for the lost time, for the lost childhood.

Semiz was careful to put the used match back in the box after having lit a cigarette, without even knowing why he was doing it.

Like a herald bearing a message in an unknown language.

The gang began to descend in spaceships from the God-knows-what unimaginable worlds. But they still felt like space pirates of the tattered and battered machinery, which constantly malfunctioned. Sometimes they wondered what it was like to be so many light years away from home.

With effort, Semiz masked his general joy, which was recklessly raising him into a euphoric mood, and the unexpectedly sharpened senses.

Even on the tips of his fingers he felt some foreshadowing of the future for that very evening.

Admittedly, there were doubts and fears that things were not quite as they seemed.

They were gradually getting used to not understanding anything. It didn't matter to them that no one understood what was happening around them.

They were looking in the direction of the first tin shed on the door of which was written: GOD!

Small gaps in memory had to be reckoned with. Basically, each of them was on the verge of anger or on the verge of tears.

They were not a pretty sight for the police, for whom it was not unusual to see the exposed bodies of the dead lying on the pavements.

CONTRIBUTE.

It was written on a piece of cardboard so that the old people might rest in peace.

Enza held that banner in her hands. Her hands were huge and dirty.

She was rolling a cigarette with them.

With hands that could be the hands of a mason's apprentice connected to her breasts, and these ones to other parts of her body, no doubt female.

There was much harmony and beauty in her appearance.

Still, she had her hair cut in such a way as if she wanted to forgo her beauty.

She drank beer in big gulps. She rubbed her lips with the back of her hand, saying "Shit! This is exactly what I needed." Semiz lost his breath laughing. In a loud, deep and joyful roar that caused passers-by to stare at him.

At that, he showed them the "fig" and they stopped staring.

Enza sat on her clenched fists. She rocked back and forth as she spoke in a pleasant nasal voice that was also casual and slangy.

They are turned on by gray hair and deathly faces.

Semiz was just leaning over that jaw attached to the death's-head to kiss her on the mouth and twist his tongue into those dimples of hers.

I knew you would get hurt, he told her, as soon as you decided to have something with me.

His words were like a mirror in mirrors, like an onion peel under an onion peel.

HISTORY IS THE HIGHEST FORM OF COSMIC ANTIPATHY IN THE DIALOGUE BETWEEN GOD AND MAN.

OR PERHAPS VICE VERSA?

Enza looked up, raising her eyebrows. She was still young and had anti-boxing reflexes.

Fuck off!

Semiz remembered the countless paper handkerchiefs under their bed, like dead white butterflies wet with the semen tears.

So, Enza, we have sunk to that level of discussion. You think we won't be together much longer! We could, if we tried.

She looked him straight in the eye before hitting him.

He reciprocated in kind.

This is why I fucking love you.

Why? - she screamed, holding her cheek. Why, in God's name?

Because we both have blue eyes.

Semiz burst into laughter just as she started crying. He didn't add anything.

He went out, his member peeping out of the fly.

She shouted at him with all her might, "Put that tiny worm back in your pants. It is a very unattractive bait."

18.

Orgasm was swirling above them and in them, taking them to dark places where they communicated with tongues. They hugged each other desperately, whispering the words mad persons say to each other.

Enza is the most beautiful woman in the world, she shouted in his ear. Tell me I'm beautiful.

Her words flew out the window and fell onto the summer streets, flapping their wings like wounded doves.

Don't get any ideas that everything will disappear. Don't get any ideas that you'll forget all this.

19.

Semiz was painting Enza for over three years. As her bottom and boobs sagged, he painted all the better.

There is a portrait of her sitting on the lid of the toilet bowl, and another one of her standing indecently in the bathroom with her foot up on the edge of the tub.

That, too, was part of his plan to try keeping her close. Because, for God's sake, she's been gone all night. He looked into every hole in order to find her. His tongue became numb, and in his eyes were as if there was sand in his head.

He was still reeling from drugs and drinking.

He was getting out of his system the torment that has been gripping him since Sunday, "If I only knew where the hell that fucking girl is?"

Probably with Willy, some metal Semiz, cool as a cucumber, answers him. That jackass picked up Enza Litzow at some drab tram station. She would do it with a dog when that thing comes to her mind. When the lady in question comes back to him, all in tears, she will know how to place her chin-wagging to him in the upper ninety. As in, she was fastening the bottom button of her windbreaker and at that moment, please just imagine, Semiz, she noticed out of the corner of her eye the points of someone's shoes.

If I had torn off that corner in time, I would never have met him, do you believe me, Semiz? Ah, that little corner of the eye, so tiny and yet means so much for a small Enzian destiny.

So, that corner of her blue eyes immediately spotted these unfortunate shoes right next to hers. I thought it to be accidental, because of the thronging crowd at the tram station. Indeed, a mass of people were thronging at that moment to board the tram that had just arrived. You're wrong, Semiz, if you think that the guy did it on purpose, as I thought at first. It wasn't that trick, like, I'm creating a space to hook up with a knockout. You are extremely wrong if you thought that by any chance.

You know the rest.

It would later be a matter of a purely technical nature. Blue eyes, so blue they couldn't be any bluer. Like a spring sky without a single cloud. Black, curly hair framed his pale face and a sad smile on his thin lips.

A prince!

He must have been babbling to you about his late mother, who loved only him in this cruel and heartless world, and for whom he still suffers immeasurably. His going through the mill because of his father and stepmother, the turbulent sea called life, and all that further setting.

Why did that operetta have to end in bed?

You too, Semiz, took me to the same place in an operetta atmosphere.

Bitch!

20.

Semi, whoa, your Enza. Enza is at the door. Whoa!
Where have you been till now?

Boyo, why are you so sulky with your Enzie? I was... I was with a fine gentleman.

With some casual fucker!

That's a terribly harsh tone. You're not going to be harsh with your Enza, huh, boyo?

Do you even hear what I'm asking you?

I have to admit that you have a fantastic nose for men. So, that gentleman invited me for a beer. Not exactly in the manner of a street boor, I must admit. The invitation was sent in a grand manner. I don't know what I would give for the two of you to meet. You would see, you would immediately like the guy, and I believe he would like you too. You have a lot in common. He too writes poems, although I think he fibbed to me. Never mind though. He read one in my ear. It's crazy, I swear on you.

What happened after the beer?

The invitation to a beer was without a hidden agenda. The guy, I tell you, was talking about his poems. He writes concrete and visual poetry. He is now in a phase of slipping a bit into neo-futurism and hyperrealism. I forgot to tell you that he also paints. He claims that humanity will understand him in the mid-22nd century. Does that frustrate him in a certain way - I asked him. No, why, that's the fate of every genius, he replied to me as cold as an Alpine glacier. Imagine.

I'm trying to imagine right now, Semiz said.

This is not so important to him, the first thing for him is the man with whom he will most honestly reveal his soul, and how much he sincerely loves people and life. There is God, believe me Semiz, he said it to me in these words.

Enza was crying with her hands on her cheeks, her shoulders shaking. And I'll tell you something else, he told me in confidence that he thought of killing himself that morning. The fact that he did not is a spark of his faith that in some corner of the world there still lives his kindred spirit.

And that spirit of yours came to him bang on.

I was so lonesome and unhappy that morning too. Don't you ever feel lonesome and unhappy?

So, as soon as you feel unhappy and lonesome, you go to bed with an equally lonesome and unhappy person. Oh, God, do you see what a cunt you are?

Semi, you don't understand that life is without an atom of meaning. Are you a cyborg or a human?

Damned beer, drums to Semiz in his tormented semiconsciousness. It always has its place to lubricate that thing.

BEER IN HEAD, PEACE IN BED.

Bummer, it's just the other way around.

Everything goes according to timetable like the train leaving at three ten to Yuma.

21.

Semiz was putting an effort to keep the icy harmony within himself.

Generous Enza, she always wanted to be of help to others. As a little girl, she used to write homework for others, buy milk and bread in the store for elderly neighbors, and as a girl, she used to collect old clothes for the Red Cross.

HAVE YOU LET A DAY GO BY WITHOUT A SINGLE GOOD DEED?

Huge black letters were crammed on the green ad, taped from the inside to the shop-window glass of the cosmetics and perfume store.

He would bet himself that Willy whispered to her down his rusty gutter as soon as she had knocked back the first bottle of beer, "You're sitting with a purebred horse. If only you'd let yourself into a gallop."

Willy is such a stupid name. It's surely written with double l and y at the end. Swabian.

He must be, a hundred percent, all greasy and covered in death spots. She really has a good stomach. It wouldn't surprise me if she spread her legs to the salamander as well.

22.

From the seventh floor, Enza observed the damp roofs below her. Streams of rain poured down the window pane. She saw a river in the distance, and beyond the river, the outlines of the woods.

Why are the woods so blue when far away?

Why is the sea when deep?

She didn't feel like having such questions on her mind. She felt some deceptive peace within herself that could turn into tears at any moment.

Her soul was like a cloudy sky before the rain.

She was not able to remove the thread inside herself, so that it would finally burst out of her and make her feel better.

The body is a diabolical mechanism.

From the blueness of the woods and the sea, over the diabolical structure of mechanism and body, on the other side of the glass, she dragged her finger towards the top to stop a winding trickle of rain.

I believe that life too is something similar to this.

23.

There is a stack of bills lying on the table that should be paid as soon as possible.

How would she find so much money?

She would have to go back to where she came from. She has no strength or stomach for that, and has even less to end her lousy life.

She approached the table. She took half a cut cigarette from the ashtray. She'll be able to drain a sip of stirred coffee out of the cup.

A whole fortune for one small pleasure.

If only everything in life was the penultimate sip. The most horrible feeling is when we start spending the last.

She sighed.

How to find a way to kindle a spark or two from this extinguished ash?

Aren't you going to keep drooling like this fucking rain drooling outside?

Go somewhere!

But where?

It all ends in getting that thing up and the semen in that thing. The rest are, more or less, lines.

IF I COULD BE STRONG and similar lines.

It will keep on raining no matter how much we have screwed up. The sun will sometimes appear in a piece of the sky and trick us into believing that life is not an ugly thing after all. As silly as we are, we'll quickly convince ourselves that we somehow got out of the shit just because we won't smell the stench for a moment.

Someone will gift us with a piece of orange peel.

You sniff to see if it stinks. Nay – it smells sweet.

Where is that little Enza from the photo in the family album? Her braids with bows tied on her head, her lace knee-highs and polished shoes up above her ankles. A short skirt, white silk panties peeking out from under it, and a hand in her father's grip. I would give my whole life for these two moments, long as much as the flash of the camera.

You wouldn't give a thing, you're not even able to take a kitchen knife out of the drawer and be finished with this crap of yourself. Rush towards the first window and fly into the air like a fairy.

Are you all the same ready for new hooks and new horizontals?

DO NOT LEAN OUT OF THE WINDOW!

NE PAS SE PENCHER AU DEHORS!

E PERICOLOSO SPORGERSI!

Though I don't want to, others push me to it.

24.

In the pocket of his shirt, Semiz still carries a piece of paper with Enza's writing on it.

Dear Semi,

I'm going to lose my mind. I know you. We couldn't break up like normal people do. I saw hatred in your eyes, but I will only remember the love I saw in them after our wonderful shagging. I feel loved and protected. I have this privilege thanks to your body, but someday I will give it up for our Ra. I have no other choice.

Enza

25.

Semiz crumpled up the piece of paper and then flattened it again. He kept saying to himself: fuck you!

He got dressed and ran out into the street.

The bus just blew past his nose. He ran the streets through the early morning, hoping she hadn't gone to another block to cheat on him with anyone.

The cold, autumn wind cut his lungs, and his heart beat excitedly.

He chuckled to himself, thinking it would be funny if he died of a heart attack.

He now no longer knew why he found it funny.

Anger. Rage. Beer. Sleeping pills.

A fat girl is crying. She came at the wrong time. If he hadn't been stoned and drunk, he would have been nicer to her. Deep down, in the gray, selfish folds of his tiny and evil brain, he decided to not wake up.

He groaned pretending to sleep and turned to the other side.

Enza was still sitting by his bed, crying softly, and he was still lying with his eyes closed, sometimes sleeping and sometimes listening.

By the time of broad daylight, Enza was already gone, leaving him with only one thing as a sign of reproach: a pair of large gray silk panties soaked in the sperm of someone's accepted lust for her.

He threw them in the trash bin and went out to buy more beer.

As he walked down the stairs, his eyes filled with tears as he imagined her sitting on a chair and crying in the dark room.

Enza, are you afraid of death?

I'm not afraid of death. To wish to die means that the heart is weary of beating.

This is all he managed to dredge up from his memory, and it must be admitted that even that is something.

26.

As could be expected, Semiz's temper began to change. For days he was falling into something he called "darkness", something that contained a terrible truth, living like a madman who fought his doppelgangers. He was increasingly losing the desire to paint. And that precisely would be the last link with reality. There, people cheat even in their dreams.

27.

Semiz was whispering to some low majesty behind the counter, who had his arms crossed, and covering those short arms were the sleeves of bombazine, almost to the shoulders, so that the man does not soil the jacket sleeves on a clean surface of formica.

Can-not! Do you understand Croatian? I am not speaking Tungusic!

I have an unemployed wife and a half-year-old child, Semiz tried to convince the two fish eyes behind the ten-diopter lens.

God, man...

The fish had an unusual voice, melodious and off-key, which matched his face. The cobra's concentric circles behind the lenses were constantly expanding and disappearing in the frames of the glasses.

Semiz saw that nothing was going to come of the day. And how could one persuade a man who was glossing a few hairs on his shiny bald head and whistling to the music from a small transistor, while he was trying to explain to him through a hole in the glass that he had an unemployed wife and a half-year-old child.

The man kept whistling the same three tones for a while and looked at his bad luck behind the counter, and then steadily emphasized, "That's the way it is."

From behind the lenses, the fish was still watching him through the transparent water. The fish closed its mouth, but "Next!" escaped its lips.

Semiz realized that the "next!" referred to the one breathing down his neck.

He picked up a pile of papers before him and headed to the lobby.

In such a mood, he went out in front of the building.

Interesting, he thought, that above all else upstairs, Večenaj's painting of the winter Podravina landscape on the wall behind that fish head stuck out to me. He looked at the lady in fur as she was filling in some form at the desk, in a standing position. She took her foot out of the tight heel shoes.

It was obvious she enjoyed as her poodle sniffed at her toes over the nylons.

28.

The cigarette was slowly burning down in between Semiz's lips while, leaning against the wall, he was idly watching the windows of the house across the street. Cigarette smoke was rising and dissolving in the air.

Still leaning calmly against the wall, he was waiting for the bus.

The bus did stop at the station. It threw some out and swallowed others.

A black jacket and a windbreaker around Semiz's neck.

The bus left.

Then a gap again until the next arrival.

He didn't care that they were staring at him.

At that moment, another bus arrived with new faces behind its windows.

It was half empty.

Semiz entered, praying to God to find a place by the window.

Enza and I are not happy when we are together.

We are not happy even when we are not together.

29.

Semiz and Enza are sitting opposite each other. There is no strength left in them to clench the fists tighter, and they both realized that it was best not to mention the problems that bothered them anymore. So many of them were there anyway that a geyser in their chest could make them go nuts.

His nails had grown quite a bit. They tortured him the most when he wrote with bare ballpoint pen inserts. His nail would then sink into the flesh of the adjacent finger. The dirt under them made no impression on him when he was eating, and since it became an increasingly rare event, it was almost natural to him.

The only thing he worried about was whether Tita would have something to eat.

She was carrying her puppies inside her.

Everything, after all, depended on his and Enza's stunts on how to get money and buy something to survive. Just enough to continue with more and more plentiful, uncertain and complicated stunts.

Tita was a good bitch. Above all, beautiful.

The only thing that could be held against her is that she had to find a lover at this time when there is not even a crumb of bread sometimes.

But what's done is done. Tita will soon become a mother, their family will increase. If there are more puppies, they could keep one for themselves and sell the others.

Tita is a purebred bitch and a noble breed. She is of aristocratic origin and blue-blooded. As long as that anonymous *adlatus coitus* of hers is not some mongrel and does not dilute that blue, ultramarine pure blood.

All could live off that dough for at least two hundred years without getting out of bed.

Enza, do you see Tita's belly, he said in a somewhat livelier voice.

Enza looked at him the way one looks at someone who has just fallen off Mars. She was looking at him with a withered gaze.

Enza, your belly has only brought us troubles. Tita's belly, you have to admit, is something else entirely. Do you get the gist of it, Enza? Tita is our safest stock. SET JSC! I will be the director general, you will be the financial and Tita will be the technical director. Fantastic idea, isn't it? SET JSC!

It is, Mr. Director General, as you say and order, mutters Enza in a hollow and cracked voice. After all, you're the General one, you're in charge of planning.

30.

From one of the hidden abysses of his memory, Semiz pulled out a pale and gray image of a pale gray and frail mother, curled up on the floor, an image that any guy in his place would probably come up with himself.

Do you remember how the soil around the mulberry tree would be purple from fallen mulberries?

Semiz silences the blind rhythm of his own heart with all its impetuous excitements and prolonged boredom.

Paula listens to Enza and Semiz going wild in the bedroom. She rolls her eyes, purses her mouth, pricks up her ears, and puffs up her lips.

And the two inside, while holding hands, caress her womb, waiting for it to flicker and blossom.

They intertwine. She wraps him in her flesh.

They giggle and moan.

They feel wonderful.

Paula watches them through the ajar door. She deliberately oiled the hinges for this petty curiosity yesterday.

She sees that they sleep the sleep of the blissfully sated.

Enza is on her back. Her nightgown is crumpled over her thighs, her face is turned downwards.

Semiz's left hand is clasped in hers.

Paula is completely absorbed in the silence so that she breathes their breath.

Sinners are never bored.

31.

Semiz woke up. He looks at the thick lips of excessively sated Enza. Sated Enza raises a strangely bent finger over her thick lips.

Does she warn him to be quiet?

Through the open curtains, the rays of the full moon flow onto her shoulders, onto her full, ironic, thick lips.

Semiz sleeps in the shadow of her thigh as if she had just given birth to him.

Is it an apparition that will disappear as soon as she touches it?

The night breeze pants through the parted curtains.

What's on your mind, Semiz?

About the image of a swallow plunging, rising and traveling.

32.

All my life she was leaving me forgotten and dusty, like an old shoe. Because of this, I was forced to move like a knife blade cutting through the wind. But even so, I felt like a hollow crying out to become one whole.

I was aware that I had a hollow in between my legs, which was never filled, leading to another hollow, which was also never filled.

If I am a zero, as I am sometimes convinced, it is because I am a woman.

It would be good if I had a good man by my side, to sleep next to me, to give me children – I would beautify myself and learn how to smile.

She tumbles over in the dark. She tries to relieve herself. From too much pain, from too much loneliness, man becomes an animal.

That filled her eyes with tears.

They are not my tears, she doesn't allow herself to turn into mush over herself, they are only the tears that pass through me, just as the urine I pass is only urine.

33.

Semiz was still persistently looking for something to do. He was not able to finish with this place.

Why he could not do it, he tried to explain to himself like this: I've been knocking myself out all my life in this Rijeka, and how to turn my back on all that now? He didn't have a single dinar of his money left.

Tears came to his eyes from the torment. Bora was raging outside. He didn't know which way to go.

He was completely indecisive. He didn't feel like going to the apartment.

He thought, it would be enough to take a quick glance from the door at those few unwashed dishes, and he could instantly make gre-e-at thi-i-ngs. It would be a havoc in the cowboy saloon manner. He was afraid that there, ma-a-aybe, he could also find Enza with a half-cigar between her teeth, and that would probably finish him off.

OH, IS THAT EVEN POSSIBLE? YES, WE ARE PROLETARIANS.

Maybe Enza is not in the apartment? The wretch is wandering somewhere.

Who knows where Enza is wandering?

Mrs. Enza.

ILLEGALLY USING YOUR SEXUAL MEANS TO WORK FOR FINANCIAL GAIN.

THE WAYS OF THE LORD ARE UNCERTAIN.

Semiz stands on the street like a dog that doesn't know which way to go. He is alone on the street.

Indeed, there is no one on the street. Something calms him down, but he feels that it will last a short time only.

Who could end his loneliness? Some old woman headed to the Trsat cemetery or to the church in the morning? Some married loner towards the nearby park? Or someone's car that, from its exhaust pipe, will stink up the ozone, the only one that still promises something nice.

He needs to get moving somewhere so he wouldn't look like the stiff dog from de Chirico's graphics. This suits dogs because they are smarter than people. Humans could learn a lot from dogs.

And dogs could learn a lot from people, not to be better, but to show how much smarter they are in imitating their masters.

Without a doubt, they are quite successful in that.

THE EASIEST WAY TO THE FINISH LINE WITH ONE'S TAIL BETWEEN ONE'S LEGS.

34.

Enza started walking down the icy street. She feels that her head has completely cleared up since the night before last.

She is ready to face life again.

Store signboards. People are shopping, shaving, having their hair cut, flipping through newspapers inside, gesticulating, observing. The old newspapers in her shoes are making her feet somewhat warm. Her thumb nail is bothering her.

He stops at the red light. The wind lifts her skirt here and there, which she holds with both hands at knee height.

Across from her, a toothless old man with dark glasses, with a visibly depraved and wry face as if snarling, looks immoderately at her legs, until a driver honks his horn behind his back.

A huge bottom and a fat face – Enza looks at his enormous beer belly – it would be smarter for him to climb a two-thousand-meter-high mountain, to sit there and feed on the leaves of berry bushes, than to bet with himself on two knees in perforated stockings. To imagine that the other person loves you is to imagine that you have exceptional values that will take the other person by surprise.

She recalled the verses of a poem from high school:

The walls are your friends,
know your walls.

- - - - - - - - - - -

Stay within your walls,
they are the sincerest love.

Enza stopped. She was standing next to a container with a defective lid, overloaded with garbage. There was more of it outside than inside. She passed the container and headed to the building behind. She climbed upstairs.

Needly eyes observed her from behind the glass. As if it were a prawn and not a social issues officer. A boil the size of Adam's apple had broken out on his forehead.

Enza tried for a while to convince him that she was entitled to social assistance and food stamps, at least as the mother of a six-month-old child.

The prawn tried to hide his impatience and peevishness because of her persistence and perseverance, thinking of the lamb within, while he was looking at her eaten-away and rotten teeth, that he could somehow give it to her only if she would give herself to him.

While Enza was convincing him that she had the absolute right to what she, for good reason, asked for, he too – a second-grade social issues officer – was pondering on and cursing at all his might the kind of women who were able to give birth to such insects, looking in vain if she was to discover on his head some kind of tentacles that were sniffing her from somewhere and revealing her hidden thoughts.

The insect tried to listen to her patiently for a while, then he pulled out some folded rulebook on who was entitled to social assistance and food stamps, and then he changed the frequency on the transistor, because he heard a woman's voice, then the weather forecast, and then his nerves got completely finished off by someone's interview on communal issues.

On top of everything, this gap-toothed one!

Enza stood leaning on the marble counter. She had already noticed that the man also had a gold wedding ring on his pinkie, which he turned every now and then with his thumb. The fellow, therefore, has his life partner, probably children as well. The fellow with goat eyes, on top of all that decor, would like to dip his little kebab on the other side, on the illegal market, to some cunt just because the fellow had the seal of state in his hand.

When she found herself on the street again, she felt complete emptiness and her floating fall into it. What had been completely clear to her in the morning was now cloudy as if she were looking at ink.

Enza tends to wander through some nondescript memories and convince herself that it could be better, but not for herself, but for the prawn upstairs, the beer belly, the stray cat, the waiter, Semiz and so on and so forth.

I wonder where Semiz is now! He's probably playing *belote* or pinball somewhere. One has to stew in this juice of life, which looks like shit soup to me. The time when I lived on one piece of cake and sent stories to *Rival* seems heavenly to me.

35.

I'm weak from sleeplessness. Without any warning, I fall asleep leaning back in the chair.

I eat badly. I got thinner, if that's even possible.

I have no beauty that could lure you. You stay with me less and less, sometimes only for the time you need to empty yourself into me.

You don't even take your shirt off.

I try to wet myself when I hear you at the door. Sometimes the fishy odor of your wife reaches my nostrils when you undress in front of me. You quickly turn me onto my stomach and do it from behind as if I were an animal. Everything in me dies when I have to raise my ugly butt towards you. I am humiliated, and sometimes it seems to me that you even want to humiliate me.

Don't go. Please don't go, I'm tired to the core. Don't you understand?

I just want some peace between us. I'm not asking for too much.

No, Paula, you said, you are the reason for my restlessness.

And you leave.

While I remain alone again.

What will happen now? I'm filled with foreboding. I curl up in the pantry. The coldness of the stone floor seeps into my bones. Cockroaches stand around me, wiggling their curious tentacles.

I fear the worst.

36.

Afterwards, cleaned up, sobered up, I'll get on the train to go back home. I will, then, sit on the porch to watch the sunsets, red-pink, purple, orange, red as blood. I will sigh deeply and lower my head to my chest and shed evening tears over myself, over the life I lived.

My knowledge smells like paints. It does not echo a human voice telling a story. My paintings are just paintings. They scare me, because they delay the moment when I will have to ask the question: Is it my own muttering that I hear from the depths?

I read my father's letter that says:

"My son, I am often lonely and loneliness is difficult for me, because your late mother is irreplaceable. Son, be brave. I learned how to make bread and cook something. I don't know if your brother is alive. Son, this is our coat of arms and our flag. I respect and appreciate the flags of all countries, but I don't know of any flag with as many flowers as ours. Lilies smell sweet all over Bosnia. I hope that they will smell sweet around the world and that thus the world will finally do something to help us.

Your father"

Oh God, I sniff my every emotion and painting like a dog sniffing its poop.

37.

I have other concerns about arguing with voices. I retreated deep, deep into myself. I huddled in the very chambers of my heart, enveloped in the pulsation of my own feeble blood. I became a doll made of bones tied together by cobwebs so that he could fold me up and pack me in a suitcase. The time comes for me to crawl into my mausoleum and close the door behind me and fall into a sleep where there are no more voices to check on and advise me.

I want to fly away with the heavenly gods.

I have always hoped that they would descend and live with me in paradise.

38.

HOWEVER, BITCH TITA WAS NOT CHARMED BY RA'S BABBLING. ALL AFTERNOON, HOUR AFTER HOUR, SHE'S BEEN SNEAKING AROUND HIM. HE HEARS HER SOFT STEP, FEALS HER FOUL BREATH.

NO, IT'S NO USE IF HE CONTINUES TO CRAWL, HE WILL VANISH EVEN MORE DISHONORABLY, KNOCKED DOWN FROM BEHIND, IN THE WATERFALL OF HIS UNDERWEAR. HE WILL SCREAM UNTIL HIS NECK BREAKS, IF THE BITCH IS MERCIFUL, OR UNTIL SHE CLAWS HIM OPEN, IF SHE IS NOT MERCIFUL.

39.

Enza suddenly grabbed Semiz with her teeth by his biceps and held it like a prey.

Make me a cow's bottom, she said. I am getting wet, no longer like a woman, but almost like a cow.

The two of them are lying on the bed. Sweat is glistening on their naked bodies.

A small table next to the bed. Completely filled ashtray, two glasses, a small wicker bottle of wine, prosciutto, bread, onion.

From the record player, in the corner of the room, a musical waterfall descends on the bed and sweeps over the naked bodies, hearts and thoughts.

Everything purls in a unique, volcano-like bathing musical medley of jazz, drama, longing, sadness, kindness, malice, dark passions and the horror of human life.

Behind them, walls with shameless scribbles. In one painting, a man in black is sitting. He was painted from the back. Fingers of a skeleton intertwined on his knees.

The man is bald. Five hairs on the head of a thick-haired man are few, and five hairs on the head of a bald man are many.

The walls of the room sway and become concave like images in the rippling water.

They ripple, and their bed has turned into a boat.

Semiz grabbed the end so he wouldn't fall,

but to his horror he started swimming, up to his throat, and began to sink.

The shadows did not stir in the least, but simply clung to the roughness of the walls, which placed their hands on each other's shoulders like the four whispering of their square plot against the two of them.

Time continued to flow in arithmetic progression for a while.

Through tears, Semiz looked at Enza, on whose face the shadow from the open window had already changed its place. Between her raspberry lips, her wonderful, eaten-away tiny teeth came into view.

As the sound of blood turned into applause, he once again felt her cold breasts and two or three pink kisses tasting like wild strawberries. Death was just shrugging at Enza in her eyes, even though she was giggling.

Someone was heard limping with a prosthetic leg outside. His steps were uneven, it could even be determined that it was his left leg that was bad, because he stepped with it using his entire foot, while with the other, the healthy one, he stepped from the heel to the toes, like a rocking chair does.

40.

Semiz and Enza are getting into a taxi because the Rijeka bus drivers are on strike today.

The city seems useless and unloved.

Some totally weird taxi driver angrily tells them, "Croatia needs a dictator. The world has gone mad. No one wants to work anymore." Semiz claims out loud to Enza that history is a cynical deceiver, that it lies to each generation that it is possible to kill rabbits, foxes, hyenas and three-toed sloths, colts and bloodthirsty tigers that have always been hiding in man.

Enza, the animals in man are immortal, he yells at the top of his voice.

The taxi driver jumps in agitatedly, apparently not understanding anything from Semiz's speech, "It's a shame that Paraga is not going to win, that Tudjman has no serious opponent!"

Semiz and Enza did not find it strange that he absorbed and adopted their world with such ease. However, Semiz did not react to the taxi driver's words, for he always lacked courage in such situations. But Enza started laughing. Suddenly, her laughter turned into a sob.

This tiny mirror scares me, she pointed to the rear-view mirror. Tell him to turn it so that I don't look at his eyes.

Semiz raised his right hand. He pointed his index finger like a gun straight at the taxi driver, "Bang!"

What the hell is wrong with you?

I don't know, he answered. I felt like it.

And he still doesn't know...

41.

It is very difficult for me to live without you. Your letter excited me to the point of despair. I guess you are terrified of something.

We should not be afraid of words when we have sensed things.

I have had enough of tears in the corners of my eyes.

42.

Paula kept her eyes shut and her eyelids pressed. She was naked while a moment ago she was saying out loud a letter to an unknown man, who was playing lightly with her nerves, with her love and her tenderness. The nipples on her breasts are pale pink. Varicose veins can be seen on her skin around them, and on her thighs. Her belly and her thighs are whitened. Her cunt is overgrown with fine and fair tiny curls.

Her round breasts delude, her thighs deceive.

While she imagines that he is taking his mickey out, she remembers a strange father of hers, who exists in her world as some shadow.

She stares at the imagined athlete wide-eyed, stupid and deaf to human speech.

She feels her own anxiety and her soul is completely disturbed by it.

This life, as it is, can only be endured with lies.

43.

I think I know a gallery that could organize your exhibition, said Enza.

The man has adversaries, and most adversaries are other painters, who are in a hurry to bury you, said Semiz. They will say, he drinks, he is married to a minor, he beats her, he lies the moment he opens his mouth, he is sick, crazy. He stopped talking, but continued to think: Now everything is collapsing! The building is crumbling. The balloon bursting.

He woke up at 5:27 am. He was still under the impression of his dream.

For some time, he lay in a state of complete paralyzed stillness.

He dreamed of a dead man. He recognized himself in him. With open, rigid eyes, directed towards the sky.

The clock had stopped and was now resting. The chairs were bored, so they yawned profusely, not even bothering to cover their gaping mouths with their palms.

Semiz opened both window sashes wide. Immediately fresh air rushed in, the great love with which people outside loved each other, and the intense scent of flowers.

He tried to breathe in all that beauty of the world as much as he could.

It seemed to him that he would at any moment take off like a launched rocket.

And he would have taken off, if he hadn't noticed a headless woman at the bottom of the street, near a barren tree. Her huge breasts (which led him to conclude that she was a woman) like caryatids told Semiz that she was oriented straight towards him and his window from where he was watching her and the sashes of which were still wide open.

The woman's shoulders, like the ones of an American football player, were constantly shaking, that was a completely indisputable fact, the only questionable thing was whether it was from laughing or from crying.

For the one to whom this dream is recounted, it makes no difference, but for the woman and the one who is just recalling that dream, well, it cannot be said that it's making no difference.

As the woman was headless, Semiz could not notice this by the emotions on her face.

But he was not particularly impressed by it.

Nevertheless, to convince himself of the factual situation, he placed both his palms on his head. He clasped it carefully as if he were at the very least holding a Chinese vase from the Ming Dynasty, afraid that it would fall and shatter into tiny pieces.

How can I allow tears when they have long since dried up in my eyes?

As before, it remains for me to hide behind words like a clown behind makeup. Semiz involuntarily ran his finger over the skin of his face.

A kitschy, porcelain cat watched him from the sideboard.

He got up. Enza got up, Enza who had been silent all the time, lying with her back to him.

Outside, a strange fog hung above the streets. Nothing like in a dream.

They got out.

They went fast as if weightless.

Above the pile of garbage next to the overflowing containers, a gust of wind lifted the torn pages of the film and erotic magazines, which others tore while secretly relieving themselves at night.

They got into the city park.

The red branches are bare as in winter. Various garbage hangs on them: paper, beer cans, tights, a shoe, a fluttering tape from a destroyed video cassette. All these things were thrown from the windows of a nearby skyscraper.

A middle-aged woman appears from the bushes. She spreads her overcoat and exposes herself.

Like from another era, she approaches as if being controlled remotely.

Semiz's legs become leaden and heavy. The body… as if stiffening and glassing over.

It really seemed to him like he was made of glass. If he trips and falls, he can break. Thus, he walks slowly and cautiously.

His feet listen to him, his head does not.

The whirl in his head does not ease off. Two hearts beat nervously in his wrist, a prickly bush in his stomach.

The pricking made his eyes clear.

His gaze stopped on the woman's oriental cheekbones.

Enza, completely horrified, steps back and stares at the white, gorgeous body with a rather hairy lower belly, and then she grabs harder on to Semiz, "The snake usually sheds its skin."

He puts his left hand on the woman's cheek, his right hand on her thigh. Enza would grab that traitor hand, but all she can do is watch the scene in shock.

What are you doing, Semi? I'd like best to take these seeds out of your eyes, she hissed.

Me on the right and me on the left, and me in the middle, he replied.

Love doesn't have to be bullets and bile towards another, said Enza.

It's because life is boxing me more and more into a corner, he uttered.

44.

This letter, dear father, will be very long and painful, both for me and – I believe – for you as well. At last, things must finally be settled between us. When I say "things", I mean, first of all, our misunderstandings, which have been going on for about twenty years and the strings of which have been pulled primarily by the two of us, with the abundant assistance of many who were around and between us and whose actions are directly related to them, which in no case can absolve us of responsibility, both individual and mutual.

But I'm not trying sfumato-shade the matter so that what I intend to say would not turn into generalization and dull its edge.

Hence let me get straight to the point.

One thing is quite clear to me: it seems to me that I will die without ever being able to determine the line, in fact, better to say the point when it all together started. No matter how much I move the beam of light to find and illuminate it, even if I circle it with all the might of my consciousness and conscience and pierce it straight with the tip of a nail, it is perfectly clear to me that this whole system, similar to a reflector, will remain unsuccessful, so we wonder (Oh, God, how many times have I, powerless, asked myself) why all this?

In turn, it was as if I didn't want to wake up from a thousand-year sleep, but rather, I wanted to turn all the way to the peak of pain and with my fingertips touch my cold heart, which often seemed to me, and I believe to you as well, mysterious and rough, only that as such I would begin my systematic inquest in the face of hellish and icy apparitions that were bringing me to the point of insanity, and by God, to perfectly crystalline knowledge.

That, dear father, is similar to going down into the icy water of a mountain lake at night, with no one around, and only hearing the sound of your strokes. There is something even more terrible and magnificent: hearing the drops falling off that arm in the air after it has just been raised above the water.

I feel that I must give you a convincing explanation for such claims, although this attempt will inevitably cause my disquiet. However, these can only be my delusions that you should completely disregard.

All in all, under the influence of my feverish imagination, which in turn had to create a perverted world in my soul, my apprehension in my earliest childhood caused newer and newer horrors within myself. I tried in every way to repel the forces of darkness and fears with a childish mixture of rejection and amazement.

As much as I was able to succeed in that in my naive and simple-minded dream, so did life around you, without my mother's presence, hinder me largely in that, and – even more – increased and doubled it in that.

Therefore, I can say with certainty that I felt uncomfortable in your presence, as one feels uncomfortable when one finds oneself in the company of unknown people.

Even today, it is not entirely clear to me why something, which is strange and unknown to man, causes such discomfort in his mental structure when it can be a possible future source of intellectual comfort and positive vibrations.

Not a single word of yours did allow me, nor action or gesture did indicate, to at least get involved in the game of guessing what could be hidden behind your dumbfounded corpse-colored character, which

I, still inexperienced, could only imagine as if it were my personal delusion.

Many years had to pass until I realized, unfortunately, all the misery or all the magnitude of my drama: alas, that character of yours was not a mask but your true face, that is, your face was an orthogonal projection of your despotic soul.

Thus my hopes that you still have one, that is, that you are hiding your spare face or several spare faces, have fully fallen through over time, and I felt so insignificant from that realization that I seriously thought for a while about killing myself.

As you can see from this letter, I failed to do that, unfortunately, which I consider (as I mentioned a little while ago) to be the misery and the magnitude of my drama, but since then my life has started to ramble increasingly.

It will also be the beginning of my complete and cruel solitude.

P.S. Don't put yourself in the current tragedy of the Bosniak people. If Bosnia is to smell sweet like lilies, I stink like you, and don't you mix these two things. It's a pity. Don't you tearfully mention late mother to me anymore. You are not worthy of even mentioning her name.

Neither loving you, nor being yours, nor respecting you

Semiz

46.

Helena Frank slipped her hands under her skirt and pulled off her panties. She threw them on the floor.

Now you take something off, she said to Semiz.

He took his pullover off, starting like an engine.

His throat was getting dry and his palms were sweating.

That still organ, lying between her thighs like a split-open plum, was waiting for him to touch it.

Helena sighed deeply and relaxed.

Semiz was lying on top of her as if on the crater of a volcano that would spew lava from behind at any moment.

The third finger of his right hand was resting in her anus, while the thumb of the same hand was in the cracked-open plum, which made Helena cry wildly. His right hand pushed her further, the hardened one penetrated more and more and disappeared from him.

Helena held her hands over Semiz's shaggy ass.

The second orgasm calmed her shoulders.

Who could confuse orgasm with pain?

They turned so that he moved under.

The sweat from her forehead dripped straight into his open mouth.

She remembered last night's dream.

She is running away from people who want to permanently damage her.

She suffers because of her mom. She knows that she is taking Dexazol. And when she doesn't take Dexazol, she takes Librium to get over the attack due to the lack of Dexazol.

46.

Semiz's soul was trying by any means to find understanding for what Enza Litzow did to him this morning, although for him it must have been too cruel of her, so he only must have felt inconsolable, because in a certain way she was at the same time both close to and far away from him so that he could successfully penetrate to the dark bottom of that painful riddle.

Frantic and frenzied, he tried to get closer to her again, touching her face with his fingertips, growing more furious and more desperate with the vague hint of what he clearly sensed. He shouted some messages to her, which were not entirely clear to him either, probably forever futile for her, and hopeless for both of them.

Then came his usual feeling of restlessness and sadness. He heard Enza addressing him directly, somewhere from the fog, "You promised me it wouldn't come to this. In a certain sense, Semiz, you have committed adultery."

She looked at him with eyes that were still glassy from alcohol and to him that look seemed to last forever.

She was sitting at the table, opposite him, and was visibly upset. This could be seen by the way she tapped her fingers on the table and nodded replying, "Humph! Humph!"

Her voice sounded sad so it forced Semiz, although he himself knew that what he was about to ask would be stupid and irritating, "What's the matter with you, Enza?"

Everything is always fine with me, she answered resignedly. That's what my biggest trouble is.

You're not going to cry here, are you? - he asked her timidly.

It doesn't matter, it's all over now anyway, she answered absent-mindedly.

I know it shouldn't have happened, but don't be cruel to me. You're not going to take away my right to another chance, are you?

No, Semiz, it doesn't matter. It's all over now anyway.

She said the latter with such fervor that everything in her head became confused. There were signs of pain and rage in her eyes and on her forehead.

The two of them were still sitting cross-legged facing each other.

She was saying something with her eyes downcast, shedding tears now and then, and which, while lifting, always met the look of the merciful. And then, more than ever, they sank into their painful thoughts.

Until then, the conversation was flowing like in a dream.

He was staring stupidly at her tiny bony hands, at other times surreptitiously gliding his eyes over her aggrieved face. If only some words would flow from her pale lips, letting him know that she despised him, that she hated him; if only the harsh words of revenge would flow from there on account of what he had done to her.

With sadness and restlessness, she said to him placatingly, "It doesn't matter. It's all over now anyway".

Semiz was thus standing in front of a puzzle called Enza Litzow. Of course, he would have wanted to stay in this kind of amnesia for all eternity, until the Day of Judgment, if she had not quite suddenly said to him in a muffled voice, "I don't want to see you again! Get out of here right now and leave me alone!"

He tried to calm her down once more, reaching across the table to her, but she was already furious, she got up from the table and shouted at him to get lost so that all the guests could hear it clearly.

47.

All day long, Semiz spent walking in the rain, ignoring it.

It's already dark.

He was thinking, a certain number of things will happen soon, I guess, some kind of a shout, and it is unlikely that I will be able to get to the one, whom, despite the darkness, I will see as a motionless figure. Although I will never reach her, I feel some tenuous resistance growing in me, against her face, her arms and legs.

I notice all three of them entwining themselves in a cobweb, the invisible threads of which are on my skin.

At that time of the night, despite the lead in his legs, it was still worth wandering about all sorts of holes and checking what Enza Litzow had thrown in his face the other day.

48.

In front of the mirror, Paula pulls on her tight vulgar orange sweater. She always wears a white lace bra.

As she struggles to get into the huge, white corset, she grumbles and mumbles to herself that she hates corsets.

She keeps on standing in front of the huge, oval mirror and a chest of drawers with a smaller mirror.

Every part of the room is reflected in them.

Paula then jumps into a tight brown woolen skirt.

Her clothes are very old, but they exude their former luster.

She lifts her skirt and pulls on the transparent lilac stockings.

So dressed she flirtatiously goes to the little town square.

It's night. In front of a nearby empty café, she sits down on a round, red polyvinyl chair.

She hears a spatter of water in the fountain. She stares unblinkingly at the round pool with the fountain. The Moon's reflection is on the surface of the water. Its thin edge is like a sickle. Since the water is swaying from the jets, it seems to her that the sickle is moving and cutting.

Is it going to cut her down?

Paula wants to order pink boza.

She drinks off a strawberry boza.

She smiles, because she thinks that's what every cultured lady must do.

She is very beautiful and still young. She now recalls that she was always extremely sensitive to touch.

A chubby blonde looks at her but passes by.

These are those touch-typists that touch the keyboard as if playing Chopin's etudes.

I'm a coward. I run away from everything.

How did it happen to me that I have always been alone? I live like a plant and fill myself with sun, light, colors and fresh air. I continue to feed myself. Once the digestion is over, the next move is shitting, and their stool is still not right.

It's the most important thing in the world.

Sperm, shit, piss, and tears. That's the only thing that happens on this planet.

49.

My love,

don't think I hold anything against you. I just want to tell you this: your babe is cute. A real doll. Namely, she is cute because she wears a mask. She got you hooked on her tight little pussy. It's only the question of her sexual attractiveness. And what you don't know is that this pussy hides many poisons. These poisons attack each penis. Your eyes go blind and you cannot see what is happening to you. Your girlfriend is crazy and she is poisoning you.

Love you

Paula

P.S. I wrote all this for your own good, if one wants to have it all good at all. It can often be tiring. Evil can often be enticing.

P.

50.

HIS EYES CONTINUED TO MOVE WILDLY DUE TO THE SPASMS THAT WERE SHAKING HIS BODY. AFTER THAT THE CHILD FELL ASLEEP.

51.

The mild April air was seducing him, and his enlarged vein was throbbing. As he thought further, he sank deeper and deeper into the realm of his dreams, and, distressed by the silence and desolation around him, he tried commanding himself to emerge from his – such lousy self – but it seems that everything remained floating above vague daydreams and grieving through which penetrated a glimmer of light and the ashy outlines of Enza that stood out against the silvery clouds crisscrossed with bare walnut branches.

It was horrible and magnificent at the same time, so that he felt himself treading the space through the centuries that appeared to him at that moment like countless apocalyptic fires, and such dimensions of time exhausted him so much that they brought him to a state of wounded pride and the insult inflicted by Enza's action of yesterday.

After all, he must have noticed right away that things between the two of them fell apart yesterday. As for Enza, she could not be said to be the loser in their entanglement, mostly for the reason that he could not by all means like her from the first moment of their somewhat closer acquaintance, and their mutual liking afterwards, while he imagined that the absence of sincerity and respect was precisely the hidden weight piece on the scale of his skill to seduce, but not knowing that she, though having considerable patience, would tire of him, and finally, well, run away.

Of course, he was not only surprised by that, but he carried things out so, again in his own way, that he felt so wounded by her action and, at first, he most seriously thought of killing himself, and because of that, he laughed out loud instantly.

How many times has it been so far that I most seriously considered to kill myself?

This was the second most serious attempt in his life to do away with himself and the second time that he missed or took lightly such most serious intention.

Some nonsense was playing in the other room.

Spring ain't here.

Blue in green.

Slip away.

Semiz then addressed Enza, "What do you think of the idea that we both commit suicide to get rid of this horrible music?"

She told him that a guy in some café complained that his wife was cheating on him, that he was lonely, and that he had no intention of shooting himself. To that, someone commented, "Listen, when one talks so much about suicide, one usually doesn't kill oneself."

The guy took out a revolver from his pocket and approached the poor guy, "Let me free you from fear, I will free you from both fear and life, and thus fulfill your wish."

52.

How can a man live on the right side of the law in these conditions? To vouch for Enza and not to swear at all if she takes off somewhere from the apartment?

To give a little money to his mother and his child?

I am reduced to a bowl of ashes and some tiny bones. There is no way for me to end my life as a man. All stories, as Hemingway said, if continued far enough, end in death.

I should close my eyes and be happy that I'm here and not there.

53.

Insomnia was noticeable in his cold, monumental eyes. The morning glare of the room.

He remembered how they uttered the words. He was still digesting the food from last night so Enza was laughing like crazy as she was lying with her ear on his bare belly. They still needed to get a lot of happy things out of themselves, out the windows, into the alley treetops where the rest of the summer was scattered.

The merciless morning light was falling on his bed. Each of them saw on the other's face the fatigue that had accumulated overnight.

The wrinkle under Enza's nose to the edges of her lips deepened.

Why did exactly their two naked bodies smell and sniff each other out of so many seemingly similar bodies?

Semiz thinks about it while Enza taps the side of the coffee cup with her coffee spoon.

It's Sunday. The air is filled with noonday bells.

An empty and lonely backless chair in the corner of the room.

Semiz, too, feels alone. He notices one banal detail: two glasses from last night on the table. Wine in his, water in Enza's. Water and her lustful eyes definitely do not go well together.

He remembered some acquaintances. Their strained closeness had to be constantly lubricated with grape brandy and such a trick, all of a sudden, seemed unbearable to him.

If he could go somewhere, to any part of the world, and not care about anything.

In the window frame, the sky was warmer and bluer than ever this year. Over the treetops, in the distance, he observed the cramped houses that reminded him of mouse holes.

From the staircase, underneath, came a shrill female voice, and fragments of other people's conversations buzzed around it, like disturbed flies.

It occurred to Semiz that the shrill female soprano could be from the mouth of a girl in full bloom who had heavily made-up, thick lips.

It then seemed to him that his heart was turning into ice. The whole event could not have lasted more than two or three minutes, and everything calmed down again.

Semiz's soul contorted from boredom. He barely managed to not close his eyelids and fall asleep in front of Enza.

54.

I would like to go to sleep but to never wake up again. What could be simpler than such a wish?

Enza is sitting in the corner of the café. Some idle drunk is shouting another obscenity at her.

Two tables away from him, a man was splitting his sides and nodding at what the other guy was saying.

You are a million kilometers away from me somewhere, she whispered to Semiz.

I am trying to understand that it is possible to be in another place, and to be somewhere else, at the same time. Perhaps I was a bird in a previous life?

Why does something draw me towards the south when summer comes?

We, who live badly, live sadly because we do not work. If you want to go crazy, some mysterious voice is telling her, go crazy.

Go crazy! Otherwise, get me out of here. Enza, go to your son!

With what! – she uttered a wail.

The word "son" was parting her mouth. It flickered in the air for everyone to hear.

55.

My beloved,
once I know I got you, I might just ignore you completely, even though I know that's stupid.
Your P.

Most beloved, since we screwed last night in my dream, I'm now completely in love with you. I'm writing you these few lines hastily to tell you the news, but the news is not good. How are you? Darling, I'm so sorry for all these things that are happening to me. I'm counting on you to help me. I wish I could run into your embrace and that you hold me with your arms on your chest like a little girl. I keep dreaming of waking up one morning as a little girl. I'd like to die in diapers. Try to recognize the only beautiful feature of the real world: nobody gives a damn about anybody else.

Paula

56.

STILL CURLED UP, RA IS LYING SOILED IN THE CORNER OF THE ROOM. TITA IS ALSO LYING NEXT TO HIM. THE TWO OF THEM ATE THE FOOD THAT ENZA AND SEMIZ HAD LEFT FOR THEM A FEW DAYS BEFORE.

FLOUR PORRIDGE SWEETENED WITH HONEY.

TITA GETS UP. SHE APPROACHES THE BOWL, LISTENING TO SEE IF ANYONE IS AT THE DOOR. SHE APPROACHES SLOWLY. SHE LICKS IT MORE FOR SMELL THAN FOR TASTE, SNIFFING LIKE A HUNGRY BEAST.

LITTLE RA WHIMPERS BUT DOESN'T CRY. HIS EYES ARE DRY AND NOTHING SIMILAR TO A HUMAN CRY COMES FROM HIM. NOTHING LIKE RESIGNIN TO TEARS THAT WOULD SOOTHE HIM.

A WHIMPER COMES FROM SOMEWHERE INSIDE HIS HEAD. HE LEARNED IT FROM TITA. HE WHIMPERS LIKE THAT FOR HOURS, AND THEN FALLS ASLEEP EXHAUSTED.

57.

What a flesh commotion it was last night! The carnal mechanics of their bending.

All that breathlessness is now becoming somewhat redundant. After that, it was stupid to kiss her with his eyes open in broad daylight.

The body that seemed so strong last night, now suddenly feels foreign, vulnerable and treacherous. As long as Enza doesn't notice, or she would consider him a traitor. Women consider it an infidelity.

He cocked his revolver and shot the guy right between the eyes. Half an hour later, when the investigator asked him why he had killed a completely innocent man – he answered most honestly, "Had I not killed him, I really would have been ridiculous in the eyes of all of us in the café who had been listening to him night after night talk about killing himself."

As I have never been able to achieve the very things that I most resolutely decided to achieve, and for known reasons, I lacked the courage and honor to take advantage of such an opportunity, even more so, I relinquished it with considerable indignation as is typical of petite bourgeoisie, cowards, and drunkards, which again failed to pull me away so that I would not continue to suffer because of my darling, whom I still could not forget.

The only thing that wasn't clear to me was whether it was an expression of my purest love, indeed, reinforced by the fact that Enza was really about to slip away from me, or I was feeling sorry for my humiliating position in such an unpleasant sentimental situation.

I should once again think of the person who causes me pain and whom I'm trying to get out of my head, wandering through some landscapes of wistfulness, and to whom I also, it seems, inflict the same, only lower and more shameless, for which I am still not worthy of her attention.

It's not at all clear to me how I can't forget her.

Why has she appeared naked in a lying position before my eyes several times?

Again, some kind of generous delusion that I accepted broad-mindedly and with open arms. I saw Helena Frank again, the way she was when I watched her in in a small room in the attic a month ago.

Is it possible that the two of us were touching each other with our hands, or maybe our shoulders? I'm not sure.

I usually believe what I imagine and not what I see.

I don't remember if we exchanged the usual, hi, Helena! hi, Semi! We looked inquisitively at each other's facial expressions. I noticed that she was about to say something, but for some reason she held back. She first closed and then opened her eyes, moved a little towards me, not changing her arrogant but not impudent look. At one point, a sudden laughter mingled with words. The two of them, well, started to go out.

Semiz touched her white skin, parted the black hairs under her armpits, caked with dried-up sweat, as if he wanted to memorize each of their shy lines; he explored with his tongue the curves and the soft earlap of her auricle, pushed it as deep as possible into her oral cavity as if he wanted to leave as deep a mark inside her as possible; he saw a tiny bit of a drawing by the closet depicting a piece of the most horrible still life, some coffins above an open grave, and all these unknown lives without big words and without big gestures; there, in the attic above the fifth floor, in the sultriness of August, the two of them left traces of the gentle sweat of afternoon lovers.

The following day, they woke up next to each other, right at the very start of day, as if they were collecting all the scattered meaning of their wasted lives.

Semiz sat motionless. He was pensive. It looked like he was recalling something.

The lack of their love, the unbearable silence fell between him and Helena Frank. He smiled at her, watching the milky marks on her eyelids and imagining the marks of his lips on her cheekbones and on her neck as if he meant to cast a spell on endless time and keep the invisible presence of another being there until the first freshness, when he would again shorten the chain to the treacherous body, and get it aroused afresh in a miraculous way.

After that, another shower, purple lipstick, a dress, earrings, a carefully drawn eyebrow line, a hymn to philosophy of life, a swaying cobweb in the corner of the ceiling.

The pathos of parting.
Behind each of their hugs – silence, bitterness in the mouth and the skin that was so nourishing in the heat of the night, and which was now losing the scent of tempting sensuality with each second.

Her body obscured his vision and threatened hell. He could live another hundred years and he would never want to leave it without her. After a month, he needs that woman's smile like he needs air. All that was a simple illusion compared to her insufficiently manicured hands, modest clothes and her calm gaze that reflected true sadness.

He was charmed by her restraint with which she accepted the conversation with him.

Thus, walking alone along the quiet alley towards his apartment, Semiz unconsciously adjusted his step to hers, as if she were next to him. Remembering those moments, he felt old and disappointed. As if he was caught in a petty theft, a smile suddenly flickered across his face. Too many things had accumulated in his soul. It angered him, in particular, that he was torn between anger at himself and self-pity. Surely, he suffered no less because, in addition to all that, he felt shame for what he had done to Helena.

With a smile of bitterness, he sat on the couch in his quiet little room, silent and motionless, like a statue. Finally, he muttered something incomprehensible to himself. For the time being, he could not expect a favorable outcome of what he had already done: as soon as tomorrow, early in the morning, he would look for Helena.

From such chaos in his head, he did not feel any calmness or peace, what's more, he was so overcome with exhilaration that he soon had to feel completely exhausted.

He lay down on the couch on his stomach, burying his face in the beaten, feathery, white pillow.

A wide smile spread to all four corners of the world.

Between fragments of semi-consciousness, he thought: a simple bird song, the arrival of Helena's letter or perhaps the warm look of an unknown passer-by on the street would excite me more than hunger in Africa or bloody battles in former Yugoslavia.

58.

From the bed to the desk, then back to childhood. It's not that far from there. It is enough to look down and see my father drinking sugar water from a glass jar colored with marmalade.

I am sick inside because I am involved in these petty things. Enza wants to dip her hands in the clear water and drink the clear, cold water.

And splash her face with cold water.

Several times...

59.

HIS LIMBS TWITCH IN HIS SLEEP LIKE THOSE OF A DOG, WITH SMALL INVOLUNTARY SPASMS ON THE INNER THIGHS.

RA IS FOUR YEARS OLD. HE IS TALL, OF STRONG BUILD, STUNTED, WITH ENLARGED ELBOWS AND KNEES, ROUGH WITH BLISTERS. HE HAS WOUNDS AND OLD SCARS ON HIS ARMS AND LEGS. HIS FLAT FEET HARDENED, BECAUSE HE HAD NO SHOES. HIS TOENAILS WERE EATEN AWAY, THE SOLE THICKENED INTO A CRUST THE THICKNESS OF A CERAMIC PLATE.

HE WAS TOO FRIGHTENED TO LOOK PROPERLY.

FROM HIS HALF-OPEN MOUTH, SMALL, GRITTY TEETH PROTRUDED. HE DREW HIS LIP OVER THEM TO INHALE SHARPLY.

AS IF BEING TORTURED BY PAIN.

HE MAKES THE SAME MOVEMENT WHEN HE GETS EXCITED ENOUGH. THIS REVEALS HIS BONY

STRUCTURE: HIGH CHEEKBONES, PROMINENT CHIN, JAW LINE. HIS EYES ARE BLACK AND DEEP-SET.

HE IS ALWAYS ALERT. HE DRAWS SLOWLY TO THE BOWL, SNIFFS IT, EXAMINES IT, TAKES IT IN HIS HANDS. ALL THE TIME, WHILE EATING, HE SLOWLY WATCHES TITA WITH HIS DEEP BLACK EYES, WHICH NOW HAVE SMALL, RED DOTS.

HE SCOOPS THE LAST REMNANTS OF FOOD WITH HIS FINGER. HE ROLLS THE BOWL ACROSS THE FLOOR AND DRAGS HIMSELF TO HIS CORNER WHERE HE SQUATS WITH HIS KNEES UP.

TITA NEARS HIM IN THE DARKNESS AND LICKS HIM.

IS IT FOR HIM SOMETHING LIKE TOUCHING HIS OWN IMAGE IN THE MIRROR?

60.

Their conversation lasted at most two or three minutes. The whole episode had only one goal because it was premeditated.

It seemed to them that they had been waiting for this all their lives.

Their hearts were beating violently.

Their clasp lasted a maximum of ten seconds. It seemed to him that he lasted too long, and to her that it was too short, so she, somewhat because of that personal judgment, pursed her lips huffily.

Their bodies were gripped by the cold shivers from that.

Semiz felt her calloused palm under his hand, the row of blisters on it, and the soft flesh under the knuckles.

You were too diligent as if you wanted to suppress unpleasant memories that way, he said.

He had his eyes shut as he said it, expecting to see her naked before him when he opened them again, but she wasn't naked. The change was more enticing, she had her make-up on and was dressed in a light, red skirt.

It was a landscape that he sometimes saw in his dreams. For him, a dream was more convincing than reality, just like the art of painting was more convincing than life.

Two ladies, both tall, black-haired, dark-skinned. However, it was not about the two ladies, but about a single one – the two-headed person. One head was Helena's, and the other belonged to the one because of whom Helena had left me.

But after some time, things changed significantly. It was already the mechanics of love and not the desire, something like an athlete getting into shape during daily training.

Before laying on top of her, behind a bush, he said to her, "I thought you might be interested in what we want to do." I would be very interested, she said. Women should not think at all but feel.

It was a mutual fantasy in which they both surrendered to escaping reality. It was indeed an admirable maneuver, although the escape was not objectively possible.

Her lips were covered in bright lipstick, her cheeks were rouged, and her nose was powdered. She had become so much prettier since leaving him that he could feel that thing of his growing and getting sturdier and sturdier. Because he didn't fully understand that sturdy thing, he was able to remain normal.

That thing continued to grow and became so sturdy that it soon became sturdier than himself, so that he was somehow too tiny for her, and it seemed that it was now some kind of a natural growth of the rest of him.

He positioned himself towards her so that they were chest to chest. Her body seemed to flow into his. They only stopped kissing when they wanted to take a breath of air.

The poet would in the second-rate manner say that they were both floating on the waves of love.

Have you ever done this other than with me? – he asked.

Of course, a hundred times. A thousand times. Just so you know, I infected them all with AIDS, she replied calmly.

The more men you've had, the more I love you. Do you understand?

Yes, absolutely.

Their embraces were battles, and their orgasm was victory. Their horrors lit up like lighthouses on the dark and turbulent sea. Their chests rose and fell faster. She was versed in speaking without moving her lips.

After a few convulsive movements of her legs, which were monstrously huge like Doric columns, she placed herself underneath him and set his thing to *cos j*, and he fell asleep almost instantly.

He no longer possessed any agility of mind. The last atoms of power drained out of him. His victory was magnificent, although she had to keep the hatred inside herself all the time.

Love made her dazed and raised her from the dead.

He was now lying like a shot quarry at her feet. There was a marble calmness on his face, so he looked more like a ruined monument than a living man.

Helena's eyes, on the other hand, were filled with blood and tears, and her face had an expression of insulting indifference.

Dazed, Semiz feels that their love has just fallen apart forever. He would love to find a solution to all his doubts in the river, but it was now so shallow that he wouldn't even get his legs wet above the knees. These thoughts, louder than a cannon shot, declared his false victory. Two flowers of wonderful colors rose before him, but as soon as he bent down to pick them, a black adder would suddenly uncoil, spraying the flowers with poison. He would look in the mirror of ethereal lake at the bottom of which two goldfish were gliding near the shore, but as soon as he stretched out his hand towards them, an amphibian monster would scare him and wake him up. As soon as he walked at night under the fragrant summer sky, two inseparable bright stars would shine overhead, but he would not have time to enjoy them because a black cloud would appear from the west and stretch into a long, cloudy dragon that devoured the stars.

61.

Outside, the sun appeared from behind the clouds, melting the hoarfrost. Things were as they had been before.

62.

Darling, I used to hate you because you didn't love me enough to devote your life to me. I should have given up demanding that you stop being a covert misogynist and sadist.

Dear God, I have often complained that the world is not fair. Now I don't think the world is not fair. Now I don't think at all.

Have you turned me into your casual flirt and a notch on your bed post?

But I have to admit: you are my world!

I wish there was a man here who would throw me back into touch with the world.

You know who I mean. Your Paula loves you.

63.

His infuriating shouts blazed like a flame. He cursed his money, her breasts, her hair.

Returning home was not easy, it had never been smooth. It is now like torture.

That evening they got drunk at the kitchen table.

Tita and Ra were growling from the pantry where they were locked so as not to bother the two of them while doing their job in bed.

And the two of them were like two pigeons on a branch erotic, cooing the treatise on Enza's boobs.

Whenever she would look at him, her eyes turned watery.

Yes, said Semiz, a good broad that I would love to grab even now.

Except that she would crush you, screams Enza, you can see it by her hips.

Yes, you can see it by her hips.

Well, monkey, I have hips like that too!

Indeed, you have such hips, but you have huge boobs.

Well, what's wrong with big boobs?

Small boobs are the best.

Are you bothered by big boobs? What you can't put in your mouth is superfluous anyway.

Honey, your boobs hang down to your knees, and your nipples are too dark. Pink nipples are the best.

Enza was lying on her side with her back to Semiz the whole time. He lifted the sheet from her body. A dim shoulder shone in the dim light. He hovered over her.

Her breasts were huge, sensual, with huge dark nipples.

He felt dizzy from the sudden lust for her. He leaned even more to caress her boob from the side. He put his hand under it, eyed it, touching the tip of the nipple with his fingertips.

And then, he reached for the dark hairs between her thighs.
Back off! – she growled.
The two from the pantry also growled.
His hand froze on the spot.
Back off, Enza repeated.
Semiz went to the toilet to have a pee.
What do you say, buddy? - he addressed his mickey.
I'm no buddy of yours, his mickey hissed, green with anger.
Semiz's head was spinning while he was shaking it to remove a drop of urine.

Daybreak found him bent across her belly, his chin resting in the hollow of her shoulder, his eyes staring at Enza's black hair on the white pillow.

A sunny rectangle spread across the bed, framing their bodies in a picture she wouldn't see when she woke up.

He thrust himself into her heat once again.

While he was drilling inside her, she was coyly stretching her arms and legs under him, telling him in a hoarse voice what she had just dreamed: my mother had prepared a dish for us made of red onions, hairs and orange peels, and we were disgusted by it, while Paula urged us to eat it, saying that it was good for a long life.

When he woke up the second time, the sun had already traveled over the middle of the morning.

The room reeked of beer, sweat, sperm, and Enza. He tried to absorb that stink.

Enza's shirt was hanging over the back of the chair by the bed. A few cigarettes scattered about from the pack in the pocket onto the seat.

Semiz grabbed one, lit it and coughed up a cloud of smoke. He immediately felt dizzy. When he closed his eyes, a multitude of stripes appeared. Blue dots flashed, millions of them.

He was gradually bringing himself to a mental state that was so above and irrelevant to hope of stumbling upon the clues that Enza's closeness brought along.

Kiss my pussy, she murmured. He slapped her hard on the cheek.

Her head bounced off the pillow almost as fast as he had slapped her. Her eyes were expressionless and wide open.

Why did you do this to me? – she asked. Jesus Christ!

Her hands were trapped under his knees.

What a son of a bitch you are!

He wanted one cruel and clear intercourse.

He was able to guess the expressions on her face for all occasions. His lust renewed itself in his frozen brain.

Tita and Ra growled once more from the pantry.

Semiz turned around. Enza's shirt had fallen off the chair. Her jeans were lying on the floor. The panties were still in them.

We loved the same style, slipped out through his gaping mouth and down his chin. We used to get along well. Not anymore.

64.

RA CRAWLED ACROSS THE FLOOR TO THE SHEEPSKIN COAT. HE STARED AT IT. HE TOUCHED IT WITH HIS INDEX FINGER. THEN HE LOWERED HIS HEAD AND SNIFFED IT. IT MUST HAVE CONFUSED HIM THAT THE COAT SMELLED LIKE ANIMAL SKIN. HE ROSE UP, HOLDING ON TO TITA'S BACK AND HOLDING TIGHT ONTO HER FUR.

HE NOW STANDS NEXT TO HER WITH HIS LEGS APART, MAINTAINING HIS BALANCE. HIS MOUTH IS CROOKED.

TITA TURNED HER HEAD, WATCHING HIM, READY TO UPHOLD HIM SHOULD HE SWAY. BUT RA REMAINED ON HIS FEET.

SHE STARTED SLOWLY, MATCHING HER STEPS WITH HIS. THEY WENT TOWARDS THE WALL. WHEN THEY REACHED THE END, RA PUT THE WEIGHT OF HIS BODY AGAINST THE WALL, BUT HE TILTED, ENOUGH TO SLIDE DOWN.

HE SCRAPED AT THE WALL WITH HIS FINGERNAILS, TRYING TO HOLD ON.

HE SLID DOWN THE WALL WITH BLOODY FINGERNAILS. HE LANDED ON HIS KNEES.

WHILE KNEELING, THE CHILD HOWLED. HE SCRATCHED HIS FACE WITH HIS FINGERNAILS, LEAVING TRACES OF BLOOD ON IT.

HOW MUCH PAIN HE IS IN, WHAT A DEEP SENSE OF LOSS AND DEPRIVATION HIS CRIES EXPRESS!

FINALLY, WHEN THE HOWLING WEAKENED AND BECAME LIKE A CHILD'S WHINING, TITA CAREFULLY TOOK HIM IN HER TEETH AND CARRIED HIM TO HIS STRAW BED.

AND SHE CURLED UP NEXT TO HIM UNTIL HE SOBBED HIMSELF TO SLEEP.

65.

After the final parting with Helena, it seemed to Semiz that he was sinking into some endless, black dream. There was nothing solid, or so it seemed to him, that he would cling to with trust and that could transfer him to the other, life-saving side, away from this one, where he had been painfully dwelling for several months. No memories, not even memories of his childhood, were a comfort to him, which could spirit him up. He felt the eternal ring of solitude around him. Every day his heart was getting colder and colder as if he had never had anyone close to him.

Of course, such feelings suffocated him and, instead of trying to harden himself by going out with his friends to forget the dark moments in their company, he was letting himself go more and more as if he was about to fall asleep at the bottom of the dark ocean.

Apart from breaking and shattering himself, there was not a single word about his intention to change something, and to grasp something firmly, say, to start with philately, to organize a family photo album of which he was extremely proud, to meet for a daily coffee with some of the remaining friends.

God forbid!

He seems to have given it all up a long time ago, and forever turned his back on what had once brought him joy and delight. Now it only caused him unpleasant memories and depression, bitterness and contempt.

Only sometimes, in despair, he would shake himself up in a harsh voice full of reproach addressed to someone vague, "God, devil!" – and then he thought that this time again he neither used the right word, nor addressed the real and true culprit.

An icy current was shaking his body, feebleness was increasingly overpowering his muscles. He was drowsy like a man coming down with flu. He felt a thousand-atmosphere pressure in his ears, and in his mind, he was still gliding the water down the calm, black abysses; a vague consciousness and a painful memory of childhood appeared from somewhere: a boy in a suit, photographed in profile in front of the mihrab in the mosque, a lady dressed in light blue with frameless glasses standing next to him.

On his cot is a doll in a white dress. His parents call him "little brother", because Semiz seemed to them unsuitable for such a tiny boy.

It seems to him that hours and months, years and centuries will pass, and he will all the same be descending and gliding in the same water down the calm, black abysses at the end of which he sensed and vaguely glimpsed the dilapidated old man, seeing a clearly ghastly expression on his face.

Sure enough, all day long, his life took place in the expanse of stagnant and dead water, and he himself was no different.

However, reality was far deadlier than dreams.

The ones he sometimes met looked like apparitions from hell.

Conflicting thoughts and feelings went incessantly through his mind. First of all, he would suddenly get the will to rush to them, and shake up himself and his lethargy with a shout of welcome and a broad smile, and to disperse the accumulated lead in his soul and body, but then, at the same time, he would realize that this idea was a completely foolish and stupid deception, even dangerous for his mental health, so he would literally be dumbfounded by it, most sincerely fearing the fact that it might actually happen one day, and that he probably wouldn't be able to forgive himself for that kind of madness, nor – finally – to survive it. That idea was as dangerous as if he struck a match in the dark and brought it close to a keg of gunpowder.

Of course, there was always the possibility that everything he had spent months creating, building walls between himself and the rest of the world, would collapse in an instant like a house of cards, because his life was already so tense that he could very easily be putting on a grotesque straitjacket, by either remaining in his proud loneliness or going back to those who still haven't forgiven him for turning his back on them so contemptuously.

Now that Helena had no longer been with him for several months, his proud hurt started to bother him, so that, instead of being more natural, his loneliness was becoming unnecessary.

66.

Enza woke up barking in the dream that had just ended. Tita watched her curiously from the corner of the room. She listened attentively with her ears pricked up.

There was something in her eyes; the manner of looking and the look itself.

She couldn't remember where she had been wandering all night. The only thing she was aware of was herself being awakened by a voice from her childhood, which shouted to her, "It's time to get up."

And she woke up.

She spent the whole night trying to find a place where her father could live and be happy. He probably wouldn't be able to respond to her hand-waving. Through tears, she saw him standing by the stove in front of a pan with a fried brain.

Do you really feel like eating? – she asked him.

She felt that he was as fragile as an aspen.

This, Enzie, is my brain, he replied. I'm in a tight spot so don't push me further with your questions.

The last thing she remembered was the heavy odor of a burnt, fried brain.

Enza felt that she was floating above the ground. Someone's voice whispered to her, "If you don't wake up before you touch the ground, you'll die!"

And she woke up. Drenched in sweat. In fact, it was a toothache that woke her up.

It has stopped snowing outside. It looked icy and horrible. Screeching tires and footsteps. Someone was shoveling snow.

The windows were frozen. The finger was sticking to the glass.

She returned to bed.

She spent the rest of the night lying down, afraid of falling asleep again.

In the dark, she listened to her mother crying and her father's voice raised in anger and despair.

I can't believe I was five years old once.

67.

When it dawned, Semiz's head was still spinning. He took a shower with lukewarm water to regain his composure. After he had calmed down and regained consciousness, he tried to remember the dream from which he had just emerged so painfully that he was amazed, after he had become wide awake, that he had not fainted from it.

Of the two Semizes, he was surely the true one he had dreamed of.

One will sooner see a snowball flying in hell than me getting any job.

It's been almost two days since he had put anything in his mouth. Mom only sent a box of chocolate flakes for little Ra yesterday.

You, Enzie, bite your nails instead of food. Eventually, you'll definitely start eating them.

Suffering is beneficial to the character. If we want to be honest, we would all have to see ourselves as strangers and cheaters in our own eyes.

Now, go to work, baby, her voice centupled with ninety-nine other unknown voices that seemed more like a growl than a friendly offer and persuasion.

In the end, only one stood out. It was saying "you" to her in a velvety voice in such a manner as if it wanted to sleep with her right away or as if it had just had the most salacious orgasm with her.

Enza got up and quickly got ready. As a long-legged and tireless mare, she went to visit some more cafés.

68.

My dearest,

I return again to the sweet scents of your personality. There was nothing accidental about our friendship, right? From the very beginning, you wanted to grow me into something better. And, I can tell you, you succeeded. You relieved me of my immaturity at the right time and thus saved me a lot of energy. I'm afraid, dearest, I don't think I'll ever find a person who will be my true friend and lover. You cut me in half, you led me into this love story of ours, where I don't want all the answers.

Your Paulissima

69.

Semiz is unemployed: he lives playing cards, gambling. He borrows money.

The man is sinking.

Semiz, on the other hand, thinks that he's not sinking. In fact, he doesn't think anything, it's all the same to him.

He refuses the job offer in a small stationery store. The offer seems to him to be on the verge of an insult, so he energetically rejects it, although Enza says to herself, "Well, we could try, at least for two or three days."

What can Semiz expect from the cards, no matter how smartly he plays and no matter how stupid the players are.

He says to Enza, "My old lady, we have completely failed. What the fuck is still holding you with me? At least you try to get out of this shit."

Enza is silent, grinning right in his face. Semiz brushes her off.

In the afternoon, he completed a painting that he had been dealing with for a long time. He is now observing its each and every detail.

He managed to perfectly capture the lustful tone of the woman's face, eyes, lips.

Enza was screaming with delight.

Both were cheerful, and in the mood to play. She kept repeating one and the same nonsense,

"When you are king and I am queen, we will have our own carriages."

Semiz grabbed a brass rod and, instead of a horse, he straddled it, running around and yelling, "I'm going to ride my queen like this, just like the ass is always being carried around so you can place it underneath as soon as you fucking want to sit down."

"Oh, thank you, Sir! Oh, thank you, Sir!" – Enza bowed deeply to him, seething with anger and holding herself back from slapping him.

"Oh, thank you, Sir!"

You see, Enza, that we are torn apart, he interrupted this inappropriate teasing. Are you up for a little walk? Just enough to get our hemoglobin working.

She said she was and joined him without reservation.

During the walk, they were silent about everything and anything, they went through all kinds of streets, he told her, Enza, if you leave me, I'll shoot myself like the greatest jerk, and she told him, in as longing a voice as possible, à la Greta Garbo, stop that bullshit, my dearest, my love, my love, echoes through the streets, squares and boulevards, whose names are hidden only in the city plan, they get so in love with each other that they become light as feathers, airy as spring, lively and in the mood for all sorts of pranks.

Now that the East has disintegrated, we're going to form a new Eastern Bloc, right, Enza?

That's right, my love, she confirmed to him, and he instantly burst into an irresistible laugh because of her bulky sweater and lace-up shoes.

70.

The smells of unknown objects in the room.

He gets up. He dares not think of the street, or start a conversation with someone.

What should I talk to him about? Should I wish him a good day? Should I ask him what time it is or should I ask him where this and that street is located?

He feels that it would be unconvincing. Do words have any meaning anymore?

Thus he prefers going to the tap for some water.

He drinks water. He goes to pee in the toilet.

He picks his passport up. He flips through it.

Where the hell to go? I don't mean Bosnia, do I?

He lies down in bed again, unzips his pants, imagines the one from last night with huge buttocks and starts jerking off.

It's crowded outside. A few chestnut leaves stick out in the window frame, eaten away by lead from car exhausts.

He came immediately, his imagination turned him on so much.

Today is my birthday, my twenty-seventh. I did not believe that I would live to see it. I have no big plans.

It was another attempt to stay alive.

71.

IN THE MEANTIME, RA HAS FALLEN INTO A STATE OF APATHY, IN WHICH HE SITS FOR HOURS AND STARES INTO THE SEMI-DARKNESS WITH HIS ELBOWS AROUND HIS KNEES AND HIS CHIN PLACED IN HIS CLENCHED FISTS. HE BECOMES CHIPPER ONLY FROM TIME TO TIME, AND THEN THROWS HIS HEAD BACK.

HE SUDDENLY STARTS SNIFFING. HE IS ALMOST MAD WITH JOY AND ROCKS ON HIS HEELS, ON THE EDGE OF THAT PEACE, MAKING SHORT, WHIMPERING SOUNDS LIKE A PUPPY THAT HAS BEEN LET OFF THE LEASH.

HE RELAPSES INTO GRUMPINESS AND NOTHING CAN BRING HIM BACK FROM IT. AFTER THAT HE GETS EXCITED AGAIN.

AS HE TWITCHES AND LETS OUT ANIMAL CRIES, HE IS NOT A CHILD BUT A DOG IN DISGUISE. HIS BLACK EYES ARE DEEP-SET IN THEIR SOCKETS AND STARE.

THEY JUST STARE.

72.

He watched silently through the window pane square. In itself, the dream would not be so terrible if there were no words at its end which he could not fathom at all.

Such sharp images within him caused terrible pressure during the day. He was helplessly, and at the same time sublimely, experiencing the anxiety caused by them. According to his recollection, the dream was very short, and it was roughly about this.

Two armed soldiers brought him to the central square, pushing him not at all gently with butts and bayonets in the loins and back.

You're turning your back on us, eh?

Whether they were telling him that or threatening him, he couldn't remember for sure, but it still seemed to him that they were just telling him that.

In the square, the crowd was pressing and heaving with hatred shouting his name, at the same time cheering the executioner, who was soon to chop off his head with an axe.

In the first row, next to the very execution site, he saw an elderly woman, with pounds of makeup and platinum-colored hair, who, flushed from her own screams, was trying to reach him with her huge thick arms, the curves of which were overflowing with fat. He clearly heard her say, "Let me get him! I will kill him with these hands!" Still not sufficiently awake and not quite clear-minded, Semiz is trying to remember these words, and he doesn't really know where he got the idea that she was the one who uttered them so euphorically, in German at that, and he doesn't know the language at all.

Her voice was hoarse like that of a drunk.

I will kill him with these hands!

Good Lord, Semiz whispers incoherently, sitting on the edge of the couch. He can't quite make out these words, for which he still couldn't be sure that she had uttered them at all.

For him, a usual state of restlessness and sadness set in, which usually came when he was faced with things he was not meant to fathom. Some unimagined threat was looming over him just because he tried to penetrate the great secret.

Understandably, the encounter with the enraged woman lasted for only a moment. He would have stopped to ask her why she would end his life, but the sharp point of the bayonet of one of those who led him through the crowd was enough of a warning for him to start climbing the makeshift wooden stairs towards the execution site, in the center of which stood the executioner with his back turned, having a jute hood on his head with two slits where the eyes should be.

As he approached him, the executioner's figure grew bigger and bigger and he felt nervous with every fraction of a second, which was otherwise understandable, considering that the few moments he took those few steps before finally laying his head on the bloody butcher's stump, did not belong to time but led directly to eternity.

That's how the last seconds of his life unfolded.

Death is such an ordinary thing, not in the least sublime and not in the least extraordinary as imagined by man. What an irony, every man departing thinks that it will be a general tragedy of mankind, even the entire living world. That very moment, the planet will stop its eternal rotation.

Everything is a mockery of man's conceit that he is truly someone and that he still means something to the space that he has been scraping for a million years like a grain of sand on the bottom of an ocean. As much as the death of an ant in an anthill, and thus, one should put an irrevocable end to it once and for all, and stop invoking all sorts of fiddle-faddle because of it. Simply, nothing can be changed there, neither for a zero to the right, nor for a nil to the left.

Inside himself, he felt vague apparitions waking up and rising. He had a dizzy spell, a sea of human heads was swaying in waves before his dimmed eyes. He wanted to lose consciousness and sink into chaos. But some unexpected and miraculous will gave him the strength to keep the fragments of this reality together, to resist and to not bow before this mob, which, roaring, asked for his head, and to focus as much as possible on what was about to happen.

As soon as he laid his head on the rough unevenness of the stump, he felt the stickiness of his predecessor's blood on his cheeks and the wild buzzing of a swarm of flies, which persistently flew and circled around his head in buzzing ellipses, fighting for each droplet.

At that moment, the executioner turned around with his arms crossed on his chest. Between his legs was the axe with a very long handle and a wide flat blade.

He took it in both hands and raised it above his head. He held it upright to the sky as if he were going to cut into it.

Behind those two slits on the jute hood, Semiz noticed his lustful velvety eyes moving as if they were surreptitiously watching through the keyhole.

He desperately wanted to reveal the face of the one who was about to take his life.

But it was illusory to hope for something like that...

The handle stopped completely in the executioner's hands for a moment. Semiz once again saw that gruesome orthogonality in the air, the executioner's head and the sky above him, and then, a fraction of a second later, in dead silence, everything tumbled down towards his neck – the axe with the executioner's hands, and the crowd, and the sky, and the entire universe.

All the universe was extinguished in an instant like on the Day of Judgment. He closed his eyes, pressing them tightly in feverish anticipation as an ominous roar carried through the crowd, "Uuuuuu-uuh!"

What's actually going on? – he thought, squinting one eye at the executioner who, in a panic because of what was really happening, swung the axe again, not as theatrically as the first time but randomly, to hit his neck with it once more, but the blade bent again as if it were made of rubber or paper.

So thought the unfortunate executioner.

At that moment, Semiz woke up drenched in sweat and with his eyes full of tears. The first words he spoke out loud were more a question than an answer, "Was that an axe that did not want to cut an innocent throat?"

A dreamed tiger can be scarier than a real one.

But, besides the dream itself, there was also a memory relating to it.

It came back to him in those few seconds after waking up.

Finally, he caught on what he would truly want.

I'd like to be gray-haired and have the eyes of a child, he said aloud.

73.

My beloved, I am sick of this lamentation tonight. This loneliness cuts like a knife, without anesthetic. Actually, I wanted to tell you about my Enza, her little Ra, Semiz and his bitch Tita, who takes care of little Ra all day long while the two of them roam around for days, so little Ra will be a well-behaved puppy.

I notice something terrible between them, but it's really a family matter.

Bitch Tita had puppies after Enza had given birth to Ra. When every single one of her puppies died, she devoted her grief and pain, her motherhood, so to speak, to little Ra who, unfortunately, had lost his mother, as in the meantime she became a real bitch after getting involved with that son of a bitch, Semiz the Bosnian, who is claimed to be some sort of painter. I read about it in the newspapers and watched it on TV. I say that all that is just daubing.

There was no order between us.

My love, what else do you want to know about me?

I'm alone. I'm eager for any man I can think of. I feel that my brain goes ahead of me, so it is watching me even now. It seems to me that, so alone, in my lassitude, I'm hovering over the things in this little apartment.

After breakfast, I exercise. Mouth, lips and breathing. Practicing. For hours, until my jaws and stomach hurt.

I know, I want to bring some order to this conversation of ours, but I sipped a little liquor, so I complicate things.

Paula

P.S. I'm tired. I put my forehead on the paper to rest my brain. I don't want to get up. When I raise my head, the paper will be wet and the ink smudged.

74.

It was tragic for Semiz that sleeping made him completely sober, that his consciousness after waking up was as clear as an empty road, so he had to drink again, but no longer with the same ferocity. He slept too little and drank too much, so many explained his subsequent breakdown as a lesson on the talent who destroyed himself. But at that time, his life had a fine and precise balance.

(Excerpts from a TV interview with Semiz Mulabećirović, the one Paula also mentions in one of her letters found in her posthumous correspondence).

TV: Let's get back to Semiz Mulabećirović.

Semiz: Yep.

TV: You have allegedly gone mad, at least that's what they say.

Semiz: Yes, I've gone mad, that's right. It is true that I will die in a mental hospital.

TV: Yes, that was also heard.

Semiz: That's right, dying that way.

"He was the best, the loudest and the most popular painter of his time, but he was never a professional at heart. Indifferent to harsh objections, he flings and keeps strong, surreal, huge smears of color. With the first one already, he achieves such a force and swirl that it is a strike on the eye. He is capable of seeing the air. He could guess by the color where, in which room, it is the freshest."

75.

The tiny light of a match suddenly sets a mass of shadows in motion. A shirt draped over a chair takes on incredible proportions.

The cigarette is used up. Peace is returning.

Will you pay me a drink? – a red dress climbs to his right side.

Of course, replies Semiz.

The red dress laughs.

You're already drunk, sweetie.

Because I'm a drunk. I want to sleep, red dress. I want to die.

Two glasses of beer at the bar. Semiz takes one. The coldness conquers his fingers. Soon he won't be able to feel his hands anymore. He'll fall asleep.

It seems to him that he is smiling quietly. He's shivering all over from the cold.

He's sleeping. He will never wake up again.

He has no one to drink with anymore.

Where did the red dress scat?

He continues to drink alone. His laughter is muffled, a wee, dejected and cruel laughter through a fogged beer glass.

76.

It's the same in the room. He remains sitting on the bed, his teeth chattering. He's empty. His despair is a complete emptiness, a strange form of horror that will never leave him.

One day he won't wake up. He lights a cigarette in the dark. The mirror across from him shows that he is no longer trembling. He has an attack of hiccups and takes two huge gulps.

He can hear horrible music from someplace and some women constantly laughing like crazy. They're telling scary stories.

The drunkards around are grunting like pigs. We are all grunting like pigs, the women in colorful dresses next to us are laughing insanely.

I believe that God is in this room. He began to terrify me.

Semiz ran and opened the door with a bang. The music suddenly stopped, the women stopped laughing, and the drunkards stopped grunting.

There was no one at the door.

77.

Semiz is balding. However, he has enough hair for his age. And that's a plus for him.

As soon as morning comes, he is in the worst possible form, with nuttily bulging balls from his eye sockets as if that of an eagle-owl.

And that's what they're called in the morning – Semiz's eyes.

Before such eyes, he puts yesterday's newspapers, already torn, crumpled, with some parts cut out.

Most likely, they were used as toilet paper.
THEY ARE SOFT, GENTLE AND LOOSE.
He reads the headlines on the newspaper scraps.
WOMEN GET PREGNANT DESPITE THE STATE OF WAR. THE NATION IS IN A STATE OF WAR AND THEY ARE PREGNANT.

Ivanka gave birth to Zoran's Ivan, Đurđa to Milan's Anja, Neđo strangled Jasna, Đevrija misattributed Fatmir to Irfan, Nermina threw soda into Šemso›s eyes because of Josipa, Vesna gave birth to Stanko's Valentina, Zumreta to Dragan's Andrea, Simon threw his children and wife Todora out of the window, Ivan will marry Marija in the Church of St. Vitus, some other Ivan and Marija will open the "Fantasy" boutique on Belvedere.
B O U T I Q U E "F A N T A S Y"
START YOUR SPRING
INEXPENSIVELY WITH US!!!

We offer you at extremely favorable prices: men's and women's colorful shirts made of viscose, cloth in all colors, cotton t-shirts, sailor style t-shirts, jeans, denim jackets, fuso pants, suit jackets and other items

> STOLEN RAIL PROFILES.
> THEFT IN THE CIVIL PROTECTION CENTER.
> THE ARMY USED TEAR GAS.
> 80 TANKS PASSED THROUGH VINKOVCI.
> MILITARY PATROLS SEARCH CITIZENS.
> A DIRECT INVITATION TO BLOODSHED.
> ARMY MOVEMENTS AND TERRORISM.
> SELF-DEFENSE OR SUICIDE?
> THE CHETNIKS SHOT A WOMAN.
> NIGHT EXPLOSIONS.
> A NUCLEAR PACT WITH THE DEVIL.
> THE UNEMPLOYED "EAT" THE STATE.
> 2... UNEMPLOYED IN CROATIA

ESTIMATES SPEAK OF ANOTHER 80,000 POTENTIAL SURPLUS OF THE UNEMPLOYED.
IDEAL MAN

E.B., born in 1960 in the sign of Cancer, says about the ideal man that, "He must be intelligent, charming, witty, patient and tolerant. He should know how to cook, provide a sense of security and admire her. He must have enough money. He must be competent and successful in his work."

Below that spot, the newspaper page was cut in the shape of a square. Semiz knows that Enza did it. He very well knows his good old Enza, who simply devours crosswords in any newspaper. As soon as she gets up, sometime before noon, she bursts into the kitchen like an Irish terrorist and caws at Semiz in her undershirt and with her breasts sticking out of the bra, putting them back in every now and then and cursing them, "Fuck you! I'd like to cut you off."

Semiz laughs like a forest spirit.

They have only one plate in the house, from which they all eat together like a true patriarchal family.

With a pile of old newspapers in her arms, in slippers twice the size of her feet, Enza goes to her summer residence on the Champs-Élysées.

From there, you can hear the key being turned twice. She pulls the flushing tank rope, swears at Mr. Mulabećirović, who failed to even flush after himself before her, so he made the whole toilet stinky.

Her favorite moments of relaxation are there, not counting those post-beer catharses.

HUSH, HUSH, MY PRECIOUS IS SLEEPING...

That is the place where she solves all the empty and half-empty crosswords, checks the validity of the filled-in squares, the place from which she screams so that the whole building can hear – what is the name of the brightest star in the Scorpio constellation, the first three letters ANT, the fourth and fifth are missing, the sixth is E, and the seventh is missing.

I don't know and don't yell!

Fuck you, you don't know anything!

How many letters are there?

Seven.

Semiz warns her to flush the fucking toilet already, because her deodorant is coming all the way to the kitchen. He doesn't know about any stars, nor is he interested in stars. He's had enough of the one he's on now.

After an hour, good old Enza finally flushes the good old toilet from the good old perforated flushing tank.

Through the noise of the water, she asks her good old Semiz, "Do you know any Kalnik-Russian name? The first letter is O, the second is missing, the third and fourth are ZA, and finally, the last two are missing?"

Pablo Picasso.

Fuck you.

Get out of there already.

Do you know how to flush that fucking toilet? You'll suffocate the whole town. It's past one. Are we going to grab any bite today?

Cut the poop, kid!

Semiz often caught himself thinking of himself being a tree, a giraffe, a stone. Or a fly.

I stand an excellent chance of running out into the street one day, in the middle of the day, and starting to shout out loud, "This is the day, peeps! Peeps, this is the right day!"

If only that would happen to me at night. That will indeed happen to me one fine day in May.

OOO-NE, ONE BEAUTIFUL DAY IN MAY,

NA, NA, NA, NA, NA, NA, NA, MARIANNA,

ON THE FIRST DATE.

OH, MARIANNA, SWEET LITTLE MARIANNA...

78.

Semiz was trembling, hugging himself, his legs and knees pressed against his chin. He fears that the time between the dawn, which he is afraid of, and the night, in which he now lives, will be too short.

Who has the right to deprive man of fear? He opens his eyes in complete darkness. He doesn't stop counting the time. His facial expression is somewhere between crying and forced laughter. He sees himself and Helena Frank, the way she used to be. The lovers had flushed faces and eyes as red-hot as embers.

She took out her bare hands, wonderfully shaped and as white as snow.

When a beautiful woman loves you, you will always do well in this world, he hears her whisper in his ear.

Her eyes were saying it, and a little later her mouth confirmed it.

79.

RA HAS A FEVER. SITTING AS HE NORMALLY DOES WITH HIS KNEES UP, HE STARES INTO SPACE. HE SUDDENLY STAGGERS, AND LIES UNCONSCIOUS. WHEN HE WAKES UP, HE STARTS SHAKING ALMOST INSTANTLY. LARGE DROPS OF SWEAT BREAK OUT ABOVE HIS BROWS. HIS HAIR IS WET. HIS WHOLE BODY IS WET.

IN-BETWEEN THE PERIODS OF FEVER, HE FREEZES. HE PULLS HIS KNEES UP AND WRAPS HIMSELF AROUND THEM.

EVERY MUSCLE OF HIS LIMBS, HIS SHOULDERS, HIS NECK, STIFFENS. HIS FISTS ARE CLENCHED, HIS LIPS TIGHT.

SO EXHAUSTED, HE FALLS INTO SOME SORT OF RESTLESS SLEEP. THEN HE SWEATS AGAIN.

TITA WATCHES HIM, SHE WHIMPERS. WHAT WILL SHE DO IF RA GIVES UP IN THE BATTLE AND

THEY FIND THEMSELVES LOCKED UP WITH A GIANT WHITE WOLF, WHO IS THEIR KIN AND WHO CAN OCCUPY THE CHILD'S BODY AT ANY MOMENT AND THEN BREAK OUT OF IT. THAT FEVER IS PART OF THE PAINFUL TRANSFORMATION. RA'S BLOOD BOILS AND FREEZES, AS IF CHANGING DROP BY DROP.

HIS STOMACH RUMBLES FOR RAW MEAT. HIS LIMBS CONTRACT TO BECOME CLAWS. HIS JAWS CLENCH, BECAUSE HIS FANGS ARE GROWING INSIDE.

80.

Semiz wandered around the city all day with the intention of finding any job. He had been out of work for several months.

Every day when I get home, I feel like I've been pulling a cart, not looking for a damn job.

All I have is one suitcase and my shadow on the wall. The City of Lights, as Rijeka is called in tourist brochures, is the city of darkness for me.

In the third street, Semiz was grabbed by three or four guys. He would not be able to confirm with certainty how many there were exactly. The matter got a bit more complicated when he found out from them that they were looking for a gun, which he allegedly hid and had on him illegally. According to the story of those three or four, the other day he had threatened one of them in a café that he would do him in with that gun.

Now give me that gun, the guy demanded.

Gentlemen, I'm innocent! – shouted Semiz as if he were in the Palace of Justice. Someone told you a bunch of lies about me. I hope you'll figure it out right away.

The guys got a bit confused. They obviously tried to figure it out, but it seemed that things didn't turn out well for one of them. For a moment, it seemed that things would be fine with him, but that soon fell through as the guy suddenly slapped himself on the forehead and concluded, beaming and triumphant, "Well, fuck me, now I know who this is! I fucked his babe!"

The matter was perfectly clear to both of them from Enza's side. Without a doubt, it was Willy. No fat and freckles on the face, no W, no double l and no Y at the end.

81.

Semiz drinks alone and paints. He paints and drinks. He applies the color directly from the tube. His brush is too slow for the melody.

Considering that he paints directly from the tube, he smears the paint thickly and messes it up. The paintings needed several days to dry.

The paintings are all over the place: in the kitchen, in the bedroom, in the bathroom, in the living room, on the floors.

He constantly cautioned everyone around him, "You're going to step on my paintings."

Most of his paintings represented animals and people.

In some newspapers, art critics frenetically wrote about Semiz: THIS IS THE MAN WHO IS NOT AFRAID OF COLOR.

His paintings did not sell under 5,000 marks.

82.

Enza and Semiz have been staring into the darkness for half an hour. They keep looking at the path is supposed to take. As they glance at the watch, their eyes hurt again. Tears from the cold air.

We must have been waiting for that bastard for over half an hour. We didn't have to wait for him before. All summer long, he was running around us like a bitch in heat. What's holding him up now?

Enza clenches her fists until the skin on her knuckles turns white as lime.

Semi, what do you think, is heaven blue?

The sky is blue, the sea is blue, everything is blue. Why wouldn't heaven be blue when, as they claim, this planet is also blue?

Even the girls in the procession wear blue and white, Enza said.

Whatever you say, Enza.

There is never any problem for the two of us to understand each other.

Whatever you say, Enza.

In her case, everything was less complex, everything was simpler and rougher. No matter how strange it was, regardless of the bright start, although not as fast as Enza, Semiz found himself in darkness and desolation. But Enza still dreamed of having a blue-eyed daughter, a Ford Sierra, spending summers at the South Seas, entertaining people, racking her brain over culinary recipes, voting for a politician in the elections, having Sheldon as her favorite author and reading all his books, following every episode of *Santa Barbara* and recounting it afterwards while having cookies and juice, having dirndl dresses, strudel with cheese, wishing to have a long life, but not these open eyes like him that are completely disheartened and just about to go out...

Cold as a volcanic lake, Semiz rolls his eyes in mad rage and envisions the image in the Islamic blue dream.

By sunset, he painted a dozen of new paintings, big and small.

After that, he walked with Enza to the park, and he's been waiting for that Fag monkey for a million years.

This is where the two of them, without bodies and clothes, feel abandoned by the human race.

Their looks are evil. Semiz himself breaks the bones in his fingers. Like a red-crested rooster ready to fight, he is angry, burning with rage and gnashing his teeth.

Suddenly he starts turning things upside down and travels through the x-dimension. He mates with everything touched by his eyes, and his demonic laugh from which chestnut leaves, eaten away by lead from car exhausts, automatically fall off. Then he begins to spin everything around like a merry-go-round does with its seats and their users. He keeps talking, talking, talking and imperceptibly begins to switch from Croatian to Bosnian. He turns to Enza, and spreads his arms wide towards her, "On your smile, I will ride into your dreams, huh, what do you say, Malčika?"

It's the same as saying that the sea is saltless, she replied.

The words "ride into" was still flickering in front of his lips. It flickered in the air so that everyone could hear it, thus it also reached the ears of Fag, who appeared next to them at that very moment.

It's best to ride in between someone's thighs with this, he showed them a little paper packet.

83.

RA'S BODY CONVULSES. IT RELAXES. HIS LIMBS FLY AROUND, UNCONTROLLABLY. HE FIRST CLENCHES, THEN RELAXES HIS JAWS. STRANGE DOG SOUNDS COME FROM HIM.

TITA IS DROWSY. SHE DOESN'T KNOW WHAT TO DO. RA WHEEZES.

A LONG GROWL COMES FROM HIS THROAT. HIS TONGUE TWISTED. SALIVA DRIPS FROM THE CORNERS OF HIS MOUTH.

84.

Semiz was sitting in the rain and quietly arguing with Enza. Enza was smitten, merrily chatting with him before going to bed to enjoy the morphine. She tried to explain to him in long speeches that the two of them were going home.

After half an hour of persuasion, Enza sat on the edge of the bed, and began adjusting her nylon stockings.

The dropper is completely full. She places the needle firmly on the skin, but it is blunt and cannot pierce it.

She thrusts harder and succeeds. Instead of recoiling from the pain, she waits with her mouth open in ecstasy, and gives herself the entire fix.

Immediately afterwards she wants another fix. She gets up and opens the drawer. She pulls out a bottle of codeine pills from it. She counts ten and chases them all down with a sip of cold, black coffee from her old cup, which sits on the chair next to her bed.

Semiz lights cigarette after cigarette. At some point, around dawn, he finally falls asleep.

He wakes up an hour later.

I feel worse than in the dream of Zenica, where I walked sad, gray and lonely, he says to Enza, to her knee, while she screams and her bright eyes roll. She pushes him with her hand as she leans over the spoon, heating the morphine in it above the spirit stove.

She kneels in prayer posture on the bed, still warming her fix on the chair, which is cluttered with ash, hairpins, cotton wool, lipsticks, tiny combs, and brilliantine.

At the same time, Semiz looks down and notices tiny bugs, and wants to make friends with them. Then he looks up at newspaper photos of porn girls in black ribbons, with huge thighs and bare – breasts.

When you have opium, you have everything you need, Semiz bleats. The whole world is then good and all of it flows through your veins, and you feel it magnificently as if reciting Qur'an by heart.

He laughs bleatingly, "Put all these paintings from the wall on one side and morphine on the other, I'll go for the morphine."

Although the fix improved his mood, so he did not reach for the bottle instantly, the morphine bewitched him. He would rather not have taken it, especially because of the weakness he feels between his ribs.

The two of them go out again like crazy. They march straight on the white line in the middle of the street.

It seems to them that the sidewalks are teeming with scum.

A group of young men, fans from tonight's *Rijeka- Hajduk* match, are tottering through the streets in the fog.

Rapaić, did ya see, knocked the wax out of Žganjera›s ears when he scored the second goal, damn.

Shouting along are some silly and fuckable girls with the bleached Niagara-Falls hairdos, wearing faded jeans.

They're insanely cool!

Semiz and Enza are getting their wacky movie through the fog. He can barely follow her.

He shouts to her, "I'd rather walk than ride this plane. I could fall to the ground, hit my face and die."

85.

Outside, it stopped drizzling. The two of them cross the street in wet, soaked shoes. In one hole, they buy an ice-cold cola and start swigging, having squeezed themselves among those who were just going over the zebra crossing at the green light.

The sky is clearing up. It could brighten up and be sunny in the afternoon. The day is almost wild, Kvarner-like, with a gray-turquoise reflection on the cloud cover stretched between the outlines of skyscrapers.

As they are making their way up to the apartment, Semiz is humming Wagner's magical music, Tannhäuser, Der Ring des Nibelungen, or whatever!

Inside, they jump into dry tramping pants and two loose colorful shirts. They go to bed with thick socks on. That's where they finish the cola, put the bottle on the table, and at the same time blurt out, "Ah!"

The bells of the Capuchin church reach them from Žabica.

People go to church now, Enza teaches him like a village teacher.

I'm sleepy, and I'll fancy up later.

Bye!

She rejects the warm kiss, the tongue and the lips, all that warm mass that makes the river navigable, and men fall off the ladder just as they were about to touch the Moon.

When she woke up, Semiz was still asleep. She wanted to hug him with both arms around the waist and clasp him with a few chosen words of sudden endearment, like "my world!"

A huge, painful face of love, which is confused, as if apologizing.

Semiz wakes up. He is also confused and surprised. He senses that this is none of her hanky-panky. He continues to play the game with her bright eyes, while she truly longs to end her ruined life in some nameless convent.

86.

It all started when Semiz ran out of morphine. Sick, he took too many Seconal pills to compensate for the lack of morphine.

He suddenly started behaving like a sloppy baby.

Enza smashed everything in the room and hit him as clumsily as she could, with clenched fists. She fell on the floor, hitting her head only because Semiz did not want to give her any more Seconal, which she had bought at the pharmacy.

She tried to get him with the bottle. He had to wrestle her.

After she had calmed down a bit, she sat on the floor like a baby-idiot and was messing around with the things, while Semiz fought a destroying dream, afraid that she would kill him in his sleep. She kept on him a pair of her wonton eyes, which smiled at him and in which there was something delusive.

Drinks don't help us much anymore, she says. It's too late, and dawn is approaching.

Semiz is sleeping and dreaming that he sleeps in the middle of the street. People jump over him. That's the end.

He wakes up crying. Enza is next to him. She is quiet and staring at him.

Enza, honey, my paintings were stolen, my money was stolen, my wife is dying, buses are trying to run me over, ah, I've never thought it could be this bad. We have become two bags of bones.

Semi, we'll only eat ice cream, amphetamines and bread, we'll buy a piano and we'll 'Chopinize' this sonata of ours. Well, I also dreamed that I woke up barking.

Semiz is not thinking about new paintings. He plays the tape of his last week's interview on Radio-Rijeka.

In the introductory part, the journalist explains that "his painting is distinguished, along with the basic thread of choosing some gruesome real event, by the superstructure and interweaving of the mythical, the fantasied and the surreal", which he believes "is not a departure from what our ganglia call the reality. What's more, it is only its transposed painful and dramatic confirmation. Thus, the art critics have noticed three leading, leitmotif details in his work so far: a miraculous, irreal dream from which no one wants or can wake up, somewhere on the edge between bizarreness and morbidness, even necrophilism, a farcical perspective on his characters, who seem skewed and their genetically coded desire to escape reality as a consequence of contempt or anxiety from it. They are not marginals, they just refuse to be the puppets and clowns in the mechanical routine of everyday existence. They possess certain pessimism and melancholy that are fueled by the ugliness, shallowness and incompleteness of this world.

Mr. Mulabećirović directly confirmed this on one occasion, explaining his creative process: in my life, I usually met those I hadn't even been looking for, while I came across those I hadn't even thought of, and I wish I had never met most of them at all. This is not just my autobiography, it could be anyone's biography, in principle. And what's a man's alternative after that? Either to kill himself, or to wash oneself. The third way out would simply be a bluff to avoid the first two offers. Everyone should have it as a joker in their pocket. For me, it was painting, which I irrevocably turned into life, religion, my physiology, a gun, an abyss, an obsessive view of Mount Everest, and what we usually call life, as something that has to be done mechanically in front of those I haven't even looked for, but have met them every day. In fact, life should be spent in a nightmarish sleep. It was only my painting that has given me the lasting comfort, I forgot about my misery and felt that I was right, although the artist's relationship with the world is sarcastically dissonant. I painted when I couldn't take it anymore and when I could go crazy because of it. I painted about my confusion in the face of a world full of anxiety, about my fears in the midst of horror, war and solitude. And after such a glamorous substitute and someone's joke about my life situation, let some future, hypothetical art historian confidently say to me tomorrow that he knows S.M. well, and knows even better who S.M. really is. His life, his characters – this is a dream from which he will never be able to wake up. He neither wants to, nor is he able to, because with his painting he carried out the *Mulabećirovićization* of reality.

And he will die in such a dream, without actually ever having lived. Thus, I would conclude ironically at my own expense with the classic ending of every good fairy tale that he is still alive today unless he has died."

87.

Paula, dressed in a tracksuit, is washing and rinsing the dishes, placing them on the knife to dry off in the sink. Then she sits down to read the business reports from "Vjesnik".

In the evening, she fancies up and observes herself in all poses and positions in front of the huge mirror in the hallway.

She goes to the table. She reads Zagorka for a while under the night-light. She has recently bought four of Zagorka's novels.

Then she looks up from the open book. She smiles. She remembered how Enza would scream when she tried to turn off the TV. For some reason, she was excessively fond of Professor Balthazar, although Tom and Jerry were her favorite characters.

When things didn't go the way she expected and wanted, she would say to her mom in the most serious way, "You know, you're really starting to get on my nerves."

Paula often played Enza the Mills brothers' records.

Isn't it great, Enza?

In the evening, Paula wrote one more letter to her beloved.

My dearest,
we could be sitting and watching old movies on TV. That's all I ask of you.

Your admirer

88.

How does it feel, Semi, when you read such a wonderful text about yourself? You're famous now, Enza teases Semiz. *Almost the same like when you're not,* Semiz answers her.

But, Semi, you're famous, and don't you bullshit me about modesty, when you've got hemorrhoids from such flattering words.

Enza, it's your problem what you think about it, not mine, and what I feel about that bunch of words that mean nothing, except the simplest blah-blah-blah.

Enza rubs her eyes and goes to the fridge. She reaches for the uncorked bottle. She pours the drink into a glass, tastes it, grimaces, and returns to Semiz for cigarettes.

I even have crack, she feigns enthusiasm.

89.

The moon was hidden behind the clouds for a while, and then it showed through, illuminating the snow, which started shining in full glory. A bit longer and the light will be lost, the wind will appear, and all the clouds, and some others along the way, will be scattered across the sky.

The sky too became brighter, although the moon, whitish, still stood and rippled over the water in front of which a man was standing. What beauty, that for a moment neither death, nor love, nor thirst for glory visit here. The water lulls even more the horror of this beauty and man's fascination with it.

He looked at the restless water and – above – the dark outline of the mountain. He watched and listened to the breaking of the tiny waves against the rocky coast.

Not only do I hear the crashes the way I hear them all night in my sleep. I want to spend the night while this is going on and draw my own conclusions.

How many more times will I be here before I die? And then everything, far and away from myself.

Once again, he was captivated by the beauty and horror of this place. *The moon and dark water are my friends.*

The howling of a wolf came from the valley. Dispelling the clouds, the moon was just setting behind the mountain peak, and it seemed to the man that he was secretly following it. The clouds floated freely over the mountain range.

The house, far in the hills, was an electric bulb, no bigger than a star. The man was afraid to go there and keep on walking.

Half-asleep, Semiz realized that he had made a mistake, thinking that he would see his mother there in a dream, and then he woke up, shivering.

Will I ever again have a light dreamless sleep?

Only now did the real confusion arise in his imagination. He waved his hands defensively as if he wanted to remove something from himself or fix it before him, but that confused him even more, so he had nothing else to do but cover his swollen eyes with his palm and calm down his exuberant spirit.

The resplendent tone of his thoughts was still active, which he took as a little joke on himself. He knew that he was playing tricks on himself by giving himself a somewhat embellished image.

He kept on defending himself and waving his hands, warding off the invisible peeves, in which he miraculously recognized some monkey freaks with the signs of night and magic on their foreheads.

Such a refined and sensitive spirit spoke in an almost colorless voice, "Was that wise?"

He was still so attached to this place that he rightly believed his words would come true if he stayed there for a while longer. His face took on the expression of a man who had something unpleasant in his mouth.

90.

Semiz "Semi" Mulabećirović.

Born in Zenica, Bosnia and Herzegovina, in 1965.

The name is neither Muslim nor Bogomil.
He was never legally married.
He lived with Enza Litzow with whom he has a son named Ra.

His mother-in-law, Paula Litzow, lives at 12 Fiorello la Guardia street.

In April 1993, Semiz Mulabećirović, 27 years of age, went crazy during a happening in a local gallery.

He was taken to the Clinic for Mental Illnesses in Rijeka.

He underwent surgery for ruptured blood vessels in his neck.

On 1 June 1993, Judge Matijašević of the District Court in Rijeka issued an order on placing him under the custody of the PD Primorje-Gorski Kotar County to take Mr. Mulabećirović to the island of Rab for psychiatric observation.

It was a ferry trip from Rijeka to Jablanac. The travel from Jablanac to the psychiatry building was done using the official police van.

Admitted to the psychiatric ward on 5 June 1993. "Dementia Praecox. Paranoid type".

Committed suicide in Zenica on 17 August 1993, after having passed by a security guard, he climbed the iron ladder and jumped into the open Siemens-Martin furnace.

91.

In the wake of one exceptional suicide
THERE ARE NO ABSOLUTELY SECURED FACILITIES

Nowhere in Japan do they issue passes to enter a factory or public enterprise, because they believe that no one is crazy to go there if they don't have to work. To enter the Steelworks – Zenica, there is still a long and arduous administrative procedure for obtaining a permit if one wants to enter and visit one of the plants.

And yet, right in the center of the very Steelworks, one exceptional suicide has recently been committed by our fellow citizen Semiz Mulabećirović, who jumped into one of the blast furnaces on Blooming. The event was a sufficient reason to be followed up, which led us directly to Dževad Halilović, the acting manager of the Steelworks Security Service.

- In absolute terms – says Dževad Halilović – there is no absolutely secured facility and it is possible to enter each one. Interests in entering one facility can be different, and when it comes to the Steelworks, it is its size and the opportunity for the plunder of public property. Of course, such visitors who have a specific goal – theft – are usually easier to deal with than those who come to one of the plants for inexplicable reasons, such as this particular case. When it comes to the case of Semiz Mulabećirović, in particular, based on the condition of his clothing and the scratches, we concluded that he had probably jumped over the fence and thus entered the grounds of the Steelworks. Apparently, in that period, the suicide victim was in a special state of mind. One of our workers, who knew him, asked him in passing how he was, as a greeting, and the late Semiz replied, "A beautiful day to die!" Of course, the worker thought that Semiz was kidding, because he had known him as a weirdo from before, so he laughed at his words, without suspecting that he was serious about it. You know the rest.

We are currently working on staffing and organizing the Security Service so that we can reduce all undesirable issues in the company to the smallest possible extent. We are truly sorry for what happened to Semiz Mulabećirović, because he was noticed and perhaps a faster reaction of the workers who noticed him and our contractors, at least in this case, would have given a new lease of life to him, says Halilović at the end.

Naša riječ, Zenica – 24 August 1993

92.

Krešimir Puc, art critic:

"*Hyperactive personality. While preparing to paint, he is constantly walking around the room. He is quiet and throws his crazy ideas on the canvas... He tends to approach the window, through which instantly flies everything he painted and causes the world to experience an earthquake the magnitude of twelve on the Richter scale. But, in all that, there is some sort of paradoxical charm. He behaves like a patient barber. He did not publicly declare himself one of the founders of a completely new art wave.*

He is a bigwig in the art painting, and he will surely have a bright future in his followers."

93.

Walter Hersch, psychiatrist at the mental hospital on Rab:

"He has a strong ego. After all, his behavior is too capricious. Extroverted, and then, as if he has swung a pendulum, he withdraws into himself. Suspicious of everything except of himself and his giftedness. A paranoid. It may be the matter of an endocrine issue.

Tendency to self-destruction. He still shows signs of life. It seems as if he is already showing some signs of death. I feel his desperate call, much more desperate and much deeper than the plain and simple act of death. He is overwhelmed by the sadness that he is trying to overcome because of what is happening to his Bosnia. It is an incredible power of reason that he illuminates all of us with. He had seen something coming earlier, something sad and terrible. As if everything he tried was in vain.

Let's be clear, it is not just about him or a few. Living, Semiz Mulabećirović speaks for everyone.

His last painting The Drowned and the Rescued confirms this judgment of mine, and after that there has been absolute silence for several years.

I can't paint anymore, he was telling me with indignation. What I do now is the insane coloring."

94.

His cousin, Nadja Mulabećirović, informed the funeral company "Dobrotvor" in Zenica by a telegram dated 4 November 1993.

I AM ASKING THE MANAGEMENT OF THE "DOBROTVOR" FUNERAL COMPANY TO GRANT ME A BURIAL PLOT AT THE "BLATUŠA" CEMETERY, ON THE GRAVE MARKER OF WHICH I WOULD INDICATE THE NAME AND SURNAME OF MY COUSIN, MR. SEMIZ MULABEĆIROVIĆ, THE ACADEMIC PAINTER, WHO ENDED HIS LIFE IN AN EXCEPTIONAL MANNER. YOU ARE FAMILIAR WITH IT THANKS TO THE ARTICLE IN THE LOCAL PRESS OF 24 AUGUST 1993, THE PHOTOCOPY OF WHICH I AM SENDING YOU ATTACHED HEREWITH.

Clerk of the "Dobrotvor" Funeral Company. Klaić's DICTIONARY OF FOREIGN WORDS lying open before him.

He reads aloud the headword of hecatomb..., and digs out stalactites and stalagmites from his nose.

It's a pity there are no more, he says, I've known him since he was this tiny.

He holds his palm a meter above the floor. It shows how small Semiz was.

On Bilino polje, that stripling used to turn over the football from those twice his age in an area just as wide as a two-dinar coin.

95.

RECORDING OF SEMIZ MULABEĆIROVIĆ'S VOICE. EXTRACTS FROM THE RIJEKA UNIVERSITY LIBRARY BROADCAST. THE BROADCAST WAS MADE ON THE OCCASION OF HIM BEING AWARDED THE VJESNIK'S "JOSIP RAČIĆ" ART AWARD, WHICH HE REFUSED TO ACCEPT.
TAPE I. 29 OCTOBER 1988

The future is sad if you fail, and it is tragic for an artist because the failure is painful. If you succeed, and the success is always on the edge of the vulgar, it is at all times a sum of misunderstandings and a very doubtful proof that someone understood you; then it will turn you into that abomination called a – public figure, and every young man, such as you were in the beginning, will be able to spit on you. You will have to bear that injustice, bow your head and continue to create like someone erecting a monument in a stable.

Only when you see that it's nothing, neither your efforts, nor your fatigue, despite all your caution, trepidation, despite all your discoveries and failures. The artist has to live day and night like a dead man in moments of the presence of some warmth such as this award, but which he neither wished for, nor does he want to accept it. Only then will I feel the expected acquaintance, who hears your cries and who understands your waving. Then I will have the strength to go on and will not hear someone's grunts.

It must be that I lost hope or that I heard laughter behind my back, or that I believed to have seen ambiguous looks being given to me.

I guess you understand that out of obligation to that unfortunate person, you must respond with some sign to show me that you understood me, but I still feel bad about it, which is the reason that I must refuse it, while not forgetting for even a moment to civilly thank for the attention and honor shown to me.

The award is a burden to the artist, an illusion is quite enough for him.

The things are changed now and will continue to change. I'm tormented because I don't understand anything. I want everyone to know that. Everything I painted and lived is a lie.

As Hölderlin said, we are gods when we dream and beggars when we are awake. In this way, I too refuse to participate in this farce. By God's will, I still look young and I believe that God wants to preserve me for something special, although I am firmly convinced that all my paintings will be buried upon my death.

THE END OF THE FIRST TAPE.

96.

I sit with this room. With gray walls that darken into the corner. And with one window that has teeth like a saw. I sit so still that I can hear the rustle of hairs under my shirt. I look away from the window when clouds and other things pass by.

I'm one hundred and thirty years old. I don't get anything. The only thing is his letter that I received today in which he tells me that he never wants to see me again. My life really has no sense anymore...
Paula

97.

In Rijeka's "Novi list", on page 27 in the CRIME NEWS section, the RIJEKA BOMBER ARRESTED headline occupied the most prominent spot.

After the explosion of the "pineapple", when the postal employee Marina Ivić was seriously injured, the police embarked on a big search. The suspect was not found in her apartment, but found were a starving bitch and a four-year-old boy, who were lying embraced on the floor. The boy is the son of the suspect and the painter Mulabećirović, who tragically ended his life last summer. At that time, the suspect was reported to have tried jumping from the Roman Catholic church. Finally, a colleague of the injured employee recognized the attacker as Enza Litzow, who had never been in conflict with the law before.

As the employees of the Rijeka Police Department announced yesterday, today they have solved another complicated case of the capture of the bomber, the unemployed Enza Litzow, who is being reasonably suspected of bursting into the Post Office in Kozala on 13 November at 7:15 p.m., and activating a hand grenade called the "pineapple", the explosion of which caused life-threatening injuries to the CP employee, Marina Ivić (24).

On the very first day, the event of the holdup case in Kozala caused a lot of attention and indignation of the public, who, together with the police, wondered aloud, "Is the bomber a robber or a murderer?" In other words, was the goal of the person, who burst into the post office and committed a serious crime, to take money from the vault, or was it the person prone to terrorism and solving matters in their own more-than-bloody way. Of course, we wanted to clarify this uncertainty with the investigators, who could not disguise their satisfaction for having under control the person who was the talk of the town, who was feared and attributed all sorts of things.

We solved this case quickly and efficiently, said the Chief of Operations, Mr. Nenad Radin. I must tell you that according to our knowledge so far, the arrested Enza Litzow committed the holdup with one goal – to lay her hands on money. We are convinced of that, even though it has been difficult to talk to her for now because of her mental state. But when a person embarks on a robbery, especially if it's their first time, like Miss Litzow's, in reality things often turn out differently than planned. That is what happened this time too. Miss Litzow wanted to get hold of the much-needed money. Before that, she had gotten very drunk. She had drunk about half a liter of vodka and a dozen diazepam to calm down, and then went into action. She kept a bomb in her pocket, probably for her own safety and to intimidate the scared staff. Unfortunately for her and the employee, Marina Ivić, that bomb exploded. It was an ill-fated Friday in Kozala...

The investigators, for understandable reasons due to the operative and further investigative actions, did not want to talk much about the operation of capturing the armed robber. However, we managed to find out some interesting details:

Immediately after the report of a robbery, the entire Operations were on the ground. Clearly, even though the weekend was upon us, no one was thinking of a rest period. And when the first seeds of doubt and nervousness started to take hold, the phone rang at the police station. A voice was heard on the other end of the wire: Come urgently, now! I have a miss you might be interested in!

98.

A paper with the following text appeared on the fax machine:

A sixteen-year-old girl, under the influence of a strong dose of LSD, cut the veins on her arms, ran up the steps of the Roman Catholic church and put a razor to her throat, cutting in deeper and deeper. During all that time, a crowd of three hundred people cheered and shouted, "Yes, yes, do it, little sister!"

The police called the cheering of the crowd "disgusting..." Everyone kept on yelling, "Yes, yes, do it, little sister! Just go on!"

The crowd also cheered when the girl passed out from the loss of blood, which was streaming from her self-inflicted wounds.

99.

Of course, after that fax message, the investigators immediately rushed to the hospital, where a new surprise, but not the last one, awaited them that tumultuous morning. In front of them was a faint girl, her arms in bandages. The attending physician just uttered:

This girl here tried to kill herself. According to her somewhat unintelligible stories, she committed some serious crime. She keeps mentioning the police. I guess she knows you're after her. In a state of severe mental derangement, she cut her arms with a razor, luckily not the veins...

Sure enough, after everything she's been through, Enza Litzow soon found herself on the premises of the Police Department. The arrestee answered the questions briefly. At first, she didn't want to answer some of them, especially the one about whether she was the bomber from Kozala. In those moments, full of anticipation and uncertainty, the expert from Zagreb prepared a facial composite based on the statements of witnesses and eyewitnesses. Finally, only then was the last doubt removed, because one witness, who saw the robber and the photo album with a photo of Enza Litzow inserted, excitedly exclaimed, "That's her! That's her! Yes, that's her! I'm one hundred percent sure. It's the girl from the post office".

100.

In a black frame next to her photo, below, it was written:

Enza Litzow, the infamous heroine of the robbery attack on the post office in Rijeka, stated among other things the following:

Believe me, I walked for 45 minutes in a dilemma as to whether I should commit the robbery or not. When I was sure of my decision, I waited a moment for the post office to be empty, devoid of people, and then I entered. I asked for money, once, twice, I think three times. When I heard the clerk that there was allegedly no money in the cash register, I took the bomb out, pulled out the safety pin and then wanted to stay there, for the devil to take me away with all the troubles that befell me. After everything that happened, I'm desperate. I tried to kill myself with a razor... You know the rest.

101.

THE BOY RESISTED, SOBBING, WRINGING HIS HANDS, SWEATING AND INTERMITTENTLY STUTTERING. HE WRITHED AS IF HE WAS GOING TO THROW UP AT ANY MOMENT, UNTIL FINALLY HE DID. HE KEPT SHAKING AND SIGHING AS IF IN A DEATH RATTLE, UNTIL HE FINALLY FELL INTO FRENETIC HYSTERIA WHEN HE SAW THE BITCH TITA BEING TAKEN AWAY TO THE POUND BY THE DOG-CATCHERS WHILE SHE WAS DESPERATELY BARKING TOWARDS HIM FROM BEHIND THE BARS.

TWO MEN FROM THE SOCIAL SERVICES HAD TO HOLD HIM DOWN SO THAT HE WOULDN'T SMASH EVERYTHING HE COULD GET HIS HANDS ON. BUT THEY REMAINED SQUEEZED UNDER THE INFLUENCE OF A FORCE STRONGER THAN THEIR WILL.

THE BOY CLOSED HIS EYES AND FELT HIS BODY SHAKING AND SWAYING FROM THE UNBEARABLE PAIN. THEY HAD TO HOLD HIM SO THAT HE WOULDN'T FALL.

HE ONCE AGAIN SPOTTED TITA BEHIND THE BARS DISAPPEARING INTO A SIDE STREET. A PAINFUL AND EXCRUCIATING HOWL ESCAPED HIM: BOW-WOOOW! BOW- WOOOOW!

IT WAS NOT THE FACIAL EXPRESSION OF A SMALL CHILD, BUT OF A DEPRAVED, SHREWD, OMNISCIENT AND CYNICAL OLD MAN.

AT THAT MOMENT, ENZA TURNED TO HER MOTHER AND SAID, "LET'S GET OUT OF HERE. I'M TIRED."

www.ingramcontent.com/pod-product-compliance
Lightning Source LLC
LaVergne TN
LVHW011729060526
838200LV00051B/3089